Eddie & the Gang With No Name

Bring Me the HEAD of OLiVER PLUNKETT

Colin Bateman

DELACORTE PRESS

Published by
Delacorte Press
an imprint of
Random House Children's Books
a division of Random House, Inc.
New York

Jacket illustration copyright © 2005 by Susan Farrington
Hand-lettering copyright © 2005 by David Carlson

First published in Great Britain in 2004 by Hodder Children's Books

Visit us on the Web! www.randomhouse.com/kids
Educators and librarians, for a variety of teaching tools,
visit us at www.randomhouse.com/teachers

Library of Congress Cataloging-in-Publication Data is available upon request.

ISBN 0-385-73245-7 (trade) — ISBN 0-385-90269-7 (lib. bdg.)

Printed in the United States of America

October 2005

10 9 8 7 6 5 4 3 2 1

BVG

For Lisa, Michelle and Amanda,
and for anyone who ever read under
the blankets with a torch.
Much safer than a candle.

Prologue

Newgate Prison, London 1681

A big, black, yellow-toothed rat skitters along a dank and dark corridor.

A cell door clanks open. The vermin run as heavy boots march past. A prisoner is marched along the corridor. We see his shirt, brilliant white against the black, but his face is obscured.

A horse shifts impatiently outside as a great door opens and the prison governor, a large, florid man, emerges into the prison yard, followed by a squad of guards. They flank a long-haired, middle-aged man, Oliver Plunkett, Primate of All Ireland. He is gaunt through incarceration, his face a mix of anger and terror. At the foot of the steps he shakes off his guards and for a moment stands alone; he turns to look back up at the prison; faces are pressed to barred windows. He gives the sign of the benediction. He's led to the cart.

The Governor steps forward to shake Plunkett's hand apologetically. "God bless you, Oliver," he cries, but Plunkett ignores him. He is then tied, standing, into the back of the cart. The prisoners from the cells begin to sing hymns in the background.

"Repent, Oliver," the Governor cries, "even now we can appeal to . . . !"

Oliver shakes his head. "Go!" he shouts, and the horse rears up, then takes off at speed. The soldiers hurry alongside. The gates to the prison are flung back and the cart emerges onto the cobbled streets of London. There's a mob waiting outside. They hurl abuse as the cart rattles past.

We hear over this the doom-laden voice of Lord Chief Justice Pembarton:

"And therefore you must go hence to Newgate, and from thence you shall be drawn through the city of London to Tyburn. There you shall be hanged by the neck but cut down before you are dead. Your bowels shall be taken out and burnt before your face. Your head shall be cut off and your body disposed into four quarters, to be disposed of as His Majesty pleases. And I pray God to have mercy on your soul."

On the gallows, the noose is placed around Plunkett's neck. He closes his eyes, breathing hard. Drumming begins. . . .

He suddenly cries, "Into thy hands, O Lord, I commend my spirit!"

He drops. His neck snaps like a twig.

● ● ●

"And so died Oliver Plunkett at the hands of the British, but it was not the end, nay, merely a beginning. . . ."

The kids at the back were sniggering. Indeed, the kids at the front and those in the middle were sniggering also. It was such a dreadful video. Here they were in St. Peter's fine church in Drogheda, Ireland, with the head, your actual miraculously preserved head, of Oliver Plunkett just a few feet away from them, and they still had to watch this rubbish crappy video before they got a decent look at the old fella.

Their teacher, Mr. Reilly, clapped his hands for silence, and the sound echoed eerily through the cavernous church. "Come on now, boys, settle down," he shouted, and clapped again. It took a while, but eventually they fell silent. "Now, boys, wasn't that wonderful! Do any of you have any questions?"

One of the boys, little Pat Rice, raised his hand.

"Yes, Pat?"

"Could you play the hanging bit again?"

There was a roar of approval from the rest of the boys.

Mr. Reilly glared at Pat, then raised his hands. "I'm sure we all saw it perfectly well the first time, Pat." Nobody else had any questions, so he turned and began to march down the aisle. "Come on then, boys, we'll take our first look at the head of the blessed Saint Oliver Plunkett."

There were thirty of them, their ages ranging from seven to fifteen, and they were all residents of the St. Oliver Plunkett Home for Boys.

The teacher led them across the floor of the church

toward a display area dominated by an ebony box which was heavily ornamented with silver. It was about the size of the top of a grandfather clock, but there were no hands within, merely a head. A dark, wizened, shrunken object that prompted a spontaneous chorus of *ugh!*s as soon as the boys saw it. It was like something out of a horror film. Its eyes were sealed and its yellow teeth were bared. It still had skin, but it looked like shoe leather which had been left out in the sun for a couple of hundred years. Strands of hair hung like straw from its pockmarked scalp. For all the talk before about the head and its miraculous preservation, they'd half expected to see old Oliver winking out at them, fresh as a daisy and ready to cure their chicken pox or make their head lice drop dead. Not this *thing*.

Pat screwed up his face. "Preserved?" he whispered, a little too loudly, to his best friend, Sean. "He looks more like a bloody coconut." The other boys laughed, and then harder again as Pat got a slap on the back of his head for his trouble.

"Show some respect, boy," Mr. Reilly snapped, then nodded at Sean as he raised his hand. "Sean?"

"The pope's coming all the way from Rome just to see this?" He nodded at the head.

"Not *just* that, Sean," Mr. Reilly replied, "he's going to give his blessing to the primate—now wouldn't it be a grand thing if we had an Irish pope the next time round?"

"So—would he have to be a Catholic?"

Mr. Reilly rolled his eyes.

"Sir—does the pope smoke?" Michael asked from the back.

"Does his wife?" added Bernie beside him. They were all giggling now, even Mr. Reilly. Sometimes he wondered if he was wasting his time trying to teach these boys anything.

The St. Oliver Plunkett Home for Boys was something of a hangover from old Ireland. While the rest of the country was lightening up, embracing the modern world, the home preferred to adhere to the old rules, the old *disciplines*. The monks and the nuns believed in prayer, in teaching their young charges the meaning of guilt, of sin, of divine retribution. They practiced corporal punishment, but fell just short of capital. It was little wonder that the boys sneaked off out of the place every chance they got.

This night, with the thunder beating through the heavens and the lightning ripping across the black sky, Pat and Sean crawled out of a top window, shinned down a pipe and raced through the sodden vegetable patch to get as far as the perimeter wall. When they were sure the coast was clear, they hopped over and made their way across back gardens, over more walls and down dark lanes back down into Drogheda. Just for a laugh.

They spent what little money they had in a small amusement arcade facing the river. Neither of them won anything. When they emerged they found that the ferocity of the storm had increased. They hopped from shop doorway to shop doorway, but were nevertheless drenched before they got very far. They stood debating whether to make a final run for it, but they didn't much fancy it. The lightning was crackling above them with increasing frequency. Pat reckoned they'd get fried for sure if they tried to cross any open spaces—he'd heard on the radio about some golfers getting struck by lightning up north the previous night. It was Sean who nodded across the road at St. Peter's.

"C'mon, we'll go and say hello to old Ollie," he said.

Pat looked up the steps of the church to the heavy wooden doors. "No chance. It was creepy enough this morning."

Sean laughed. "Better than standing here," he said, then without another word darted out into the rain, and across the road toward the church.

"Sean!"

But he was away up the steps already.

Pat waited in the shadows for a car to pass, then hurried across after his friend. He called after him again, but Sean had already opened the door and disappeared inside. For some reason they never locked church doors. Which was pretty stupid, Pat thought. It was asking for trouble, particularly from boys like him and Sean. Pat took the steps three at a time. He paused at the partially open door, glanced back at the empty road, then crossed himself and entered.

He shivered. He didn't like this one bit. The lights were off, leaving the church lit only by the meager flames of a dozen candles at the back table and a small lamp near the front that illuminated the glass case and the wooden box behind it in which sat the sacred head of Saint Oliver Plunkett.

Pat pushed the door closed behind him. He whispered Sean's name, but there was no response. The candle flames, enticed by a hundred drafts, threw curious dancing shadows across the walls. The air smelled of wax and funerals.

Pat slowly padded down the aisle, whispering Sean's name as he went. As he approached the altar, Pat didn't have the nerve to look at the head, so instead he focused on the stained-glass window ahead of him. The Virgin Mary. He crossed himself again, then turned to look back down the aisle to see if there was any sign of his friend.

"Looking for someone?" Sean said, stepping suddenly out of the shadows.

Pat let out a yell. "Don't do that!"

He tried to slap Sean round the head, but Sean ducked under his hand and was off and running and laughing. Pat chased after him, and they were soon giggling and shouting and wrestling and climbing all over the pews.

After a while they paused to catch their breath. Sean stood looking at the ancient head. Pat hung back by the front row of pews.

Sean waved him forward. "Come on," he said, "what're you scared of?"

Pat ventured cautiously forward, almost on tiptoes. He raised his eyebrows at Sean, then finally turned his eyes on the blessed saint. Immediately another shiver ran through him. "Uuuuugh!" Then, a little embarrassed at his reaction, he added quickly: "He looks like your da."

"He looks like your ma."

"He looks like your girlfriend's bum."

"At least I have a girlfriend."

In fact, he didn't. Neither did Pat. Nor parents. They were orphans both.

Pat, growing a little more used to the head, bent forward and stared through the glass. He raised his fingers and gently placed them against the cool glass. He began to trace the outline of the ancient head.

A loud crack echoed suddenly through the church. They both jumped. Pat stared horrified at the glass case, thinking he'd somehow managed to crack it, but then Sean grabbed his arm and pulled him quickly to one side, out of the light. They scurried along as far as the third aisle, then threw themselves to the floor. Pat started to say something, but Sean shushed him, then cautiously raised himself. The church door was open, and three figures stood at the top of the center aisle. Sean ducked down again as the beam of a high-powered torch licked out over the top of the pews. They pressed themselves into the cold stone floor. Heavy footsteps sounded along the aisle and Pat screwed his eyes tight shut and prayed that they wouldn't be discovered. Sean, a little braver, saw heavy black boots pass by the end of their row.

With his immediate surroundings returned to near darkness, Sean raised himself just a fraction. He could see that the three men were wearing dark overalls and had balaclavas pulled down over their faces. They were grouped around the ebony and silver case containing the head of Oliver Plunkett. They spoke in hushed tones. The light from the candles threw giant silhouettes of them across the church walls. There came a metallic snapping sound. There was another snap, then another, and finally a fourth.

The men lifted the case containing the head of Oliver Plunkett from its base. Two of them carried it up the aisle; the third came up behind, his torch raking the darkness. They reached the doors, then hesitated for a moment before hurrying back out into the howling gale.

Sean looked at Pat. Even in the darkness Pat's eyes seemed huge and frightened. He was shaking. Sean pulled him by the arm. "Come on," he said, "we'll find another way out. Sooner we flit from here the better." But Pat wouldn't budge. "C'mon, Pat," he said, and pulled at his arm again, but Pat shook himself free. His mind was racing as fast as his heart. They'd stolen the head of Oliver Plunkett! And he hadn't done anything to stop them.

Abruptly he turned away from his friend and began to hurry back up the center aisle. Before he was halfway he started running.

"Pat! What're you doing! What if . . ."

But Pat wasn't listening, he had reached the great wooden door. He charged through the gap, then skidded to a halt outside just as a car pulled out from the curb, its wipers already working hard against the torrential rain.

A moment later Sean arrived at his shoulder. Pat turned, his face flushed with excitement and rain. "We have to call the police. We have to call the Guards!"

But Sean was having none of it. He grabbed Pat by the

shirt and slammed him against the church door. "Are you mental or something?" he shouted. "We didn't see any-thing, okay? We're home in bed tucked up, all right?"

"But—"

"But nothing! They find out we were here, the priests will skin us alive!"

Pat took a deep breath, then looked back out into the rain. The car was gone. The street was empty. He glanced back into the church. It too felt empty. And something more—desecrated. He didn't know where the word sprang from, and he certainly couldn't spell it, but it was absolutely the right word. Desecrated.

One

Eddie Malone had great plans for world domination.

There were already vast and scary gangs out there, making billions of pounds every week—the Mafia in Italy and America, the Yakuza in Japan, the fearsome Russian mobs—but Eddie's outfit would put them all in the shade. He would control the cities, the streets, the people, he would be a man capable of great anger, great violence, but also of great kindness. He would be respected. He would do good things, and when he had to, bad things. He would be a Godfather to the whole world, a friend who you didn't necessarily want to hang around with or go to the movies with, but one who you could call on in times of need, who could solve your problems in the way a normal friend, or a parent, or a cop, couldn't. And at the right price.

In fact, the only thing that stood between Eddie Malone and complete and utter world domination was the fact that his was a Gang of One. Eddie Malone was the leader of a gang which had no members, apart from himself.

Eddie Malone did not dominate the world.

He did not dominate his country.

He did not dominate his city.

Or even his street.

In fact most of the time he did not even dominate his apartment, which was on the seventeenth floor of the nurses' building, right next door to the vast and gloomy Royal Victoria Hospital. The apartment was usually the domain of his mother. When she wasn't there Eddie ruled it with absolute authority, as long as he didn't make a mess, have the music up too loud or spend too much time on the Internet. Eddie's father had run off with Spaghetti Legs several months before, and hadn't been heard from since. Although Eddie now lived under a strict set of instructions, dictated by his mother as if she was God giving Moses the Ten Commandments, he barely paid any attention to them, unless she was watching or within shouting distance. Who did she think she was? Hadn't he saved the lives of a dozen little babies just a few weeks before? Hadn't he been photographed by national newspapers and described as a hero by famous television personalities? And her rules were *so* ridiculous. Don't do this, don't do that, don't do this, don't do that.

Eddie broke every single one of them.

In his head, at least.

The problem was, he was more or less a prisoner in his own home. After performing such heroics against the now-in-prison baby-snatchers, Eddie had expected to be carried through the streets on people's shoulders; he had expected that all the local kids would flock to join his gang; he had expected that his young albino friend Mo would be at his side, coming up with bright ideas for making money or pulling scams or at the very least raiding the territory of their archrivals, the Reservoir Pups. But as many people have found, there is nothing as old as yesterday's news. The day after he'd been declared a hero, a war had broken out somewhere, as they always do, and suddenly nobody could remember how important Eddie was, or indeed, who he was. The Reservoir Pups, under Captain Black, had cheated Eddie out of the reward money for saving the babies and now seemed to be going from strength to strength on the back of it. Certainly Eddie could hardly leave the apartment block without being chased by Pups; he had been beaten up twice. Even when he did eventually meet some kid who had even fewer friends than he had, or who had some vague memory of the famous person he might once fleetingly have been, and who wasn't already a member of any gang, they would run a mile when Eddie suggested helping him form a gang. To Eddie it seemed clear that there was something about him that said: run away quick, danger lies this way.

Eddie could no longer even explore the hospital next door. Security had been trebled since the twelve babies had been kidnapped—now he was lucky if the big black boots of Chief of Security Bernard Scuttles didn't kick out at him within a minute of his stepping inside the hospital. Scuttles, who had played some minor role in the recovery of the babies, now fancied himself something of a superhero. He wore a uniform rich with gold braid and shiny with metal buttons and fake medals; if you hadn't known he was merely a security guard you might have imagined he was the president of a small South American country come to visit the hospital.

So Eddie couldn't go out on the streets, he couldn't roam the hospital.

Eddie was bored, bored, bored, bored, bored.

He was supposed to be leading a dynamic new gang with Mo—but he hadn't seen her in weeks; indeed he might never see her again.

Mo was an Albino by name, and an albino by nature. When he had first met her she was a member of the infamous Andytown Albinos, a fearsome outfit which even scared the pants off the Reservoir Pups. It was only by chance that Eddie found out that the Andytown Albinos consisted of precisely one member—Mo, a white-haired, white-skinned, decidedly odd-looking little girl who was so adept at causing trouble that she had fooled an entire city full of violent gangs into thinking that her outfit was more dangerous than all the rest.

Eddie still wasn't quite sure how to feel about Mo.

She was odd looking. Quite pretty, he supposed, but only if you were looking for that sort of thing, as opposed to an ally with whom to plan world domination.

Although they'd fought a lot at the start, she was good fun to be with. But she was the sort of friend you didn't mind having, as long as your other, regular friends didn't find out about her.

Although, of course, Eddie didn't have any other friends.

He had even introduced her to his mum. She was a nurse and by all accounts a very good and caring one, much loved by her patients, but she really didn't know what to make of Mo. She sensed trouble and advised Eddie to find some friends of his own "type." Eddie wasn't quite sure what his mum meant by type because she quickly changed the subject, but he supposed she meant "someone a bit more normal looking, whose dad isn't in prison for shooting people."

That was understandable, he supposed, except of course that Mo's dad was no longer in prison—and that turned out to be the whole problem.

All sorts of murderers and killers and robbers— although thankfully not the baby-snatchers—had been released from prison recently as long as they promised to be good. Eddie thought this was ridiculous, asking people who told lies as a matter of course, to promise to be good, but he had long since given up trying to work out the ways of the adult world. His world was hard enough. And he had been happy for Mo when she had bounced round to his apartment one night to tell him her dad was getting out of prison. He had been happy, but he had concealed it with a gruff "Well, I hope he doesn't think he's going to interfere with our plans," and she'd looked a bit disappointed with that—but what did he care, he was the

15

leader of a gang bent on world domination, and they didn't even have a name yet. How were they supposed to create fear and havoc without the right name? There were so many things to do, he couldn't have Mo running off to play happy families with her dad.

Mostly, he supposed he was so mean because *he* didn't have a dad to run off with.

His dad, somewhere in England with Spaghetti Legs, still hadn't called him, or written to him, or sent him a birthday present. He had run off with his new love without so much as a hug or a kiss on the forehead. Just gone. Like that.

After Mo left to be with her dad he regretted being mean. Kind of. He was still trying to think big brave thoughts like, you gotta be mean to survive in this rough tough world of ours. Those kinds of thoughts were fine, but they could mean that you spent a lot of time by yourself. Eddie didn't quite know what to do with himself when Mo failed to appear for the next scheduled meeting of their new gang. It was really frustrating—he had finally drawn up a whole list of possible names for his— sorry, their—gang, names that sounded dangerous, but quite witty as well. He was sure Mo would be impressed.

But she didn't appear.

Nor did she turn up to explain herself later, or at any time during the next five days.

It was nothing less than mutiny. Or treason.

More importantly, it was really annoying.

Eddie pretended he had big important things to be

doing, that it didn't matter to him whether she turned up, but his annoyance grew with each passing day. In fact, minute. He had a curious empty feeling in his stomach, which he tried to fill by stealing his mother's Jaffa cakes. But she was wise to his ways by now and kept them under lock and key. He had to make do with stale biscuits.

So, no show Mo.

Well, tough.

Tough on her.

Who needs her?

Who needs a girl?

Who needs a funny-looking albino for a friend?

I've got lots of other friends—

Like . . .

Like . . .

Oh yeah, like the man who washes the bodies in the mortuary. Barney.

Except Eddie hadn't been able to see him either, because of all the security at the hospital.

So Eddie went for a walk.

If it meant risking life and limb by passing through the territory of the Reservoir Pups, well, he was still just going for a walk. If it eventually took him to the territory formerly controlled by the Andytown Albinos, well, that was just a coincidence. And if he happened to pass by the house where Mo was living with her dad, well, that was . . . fate.

And perhaps fate was on his side, because the day he

decided to walk to Mo's house, he wasn't beaten up once. Nor chased. Nor called all the names of the day. It was a lovely late summer's morning. He wore a T-shirt, black jeans, baseball boots; his hair was cut short, but it certainly wasn't a crew cut; he'd tried to get one, but Mum had overruled. How tough was that? He wanted a crew cut, but Mummy wouldn't let him. He could just picture his friends chanting it. *But Mummy wouldn't let me! But Mummy wouldn't let me!*

Except, of course, that he didn't have any friends.

So he knocked on Mo's door and tried to act all cool and casual. Except it wasn't Mo that answered it but her dad, a big man in a vest, with tattoos on his arms, who looked at Eddie like he'd come to collect a bad debt.

"What?" he snapped.

"Is Mo in?"

"No. And who the hell are you?"

"Eddie. Eddie Malone."

Her dad peered at him a little closer and sneered: "Right. Eddie Malone. The big hero." Except he didn't say "hero" like it was a good thing; he made it sound like Eddie was a clown or a fool.

Eddie just kind of shrugged. "She's not in, then?"

"Isn't that what I bloody said?" her dad barked.

"Yes . . . sorry, when will she be . . . ?"

"She won't."

Eddie was stunned. "She, I mean . . . where . . . ?"

"She's gone to live with her uncle in Scotland, all right? I'm just out of prison, all right? They don't think

I'm responsible enough to look after my own daughter, okay? So they made me pack her off to her relatives, or they'd put her in a home, all right?"

Mo's dad was snapping angrily, but he also looked like he was about to cry.

"She's gone?"

"Yes she's gone! Don't you listen, cloth ears?"

"Yes . . . but . . . she . . . she and I were . . ."

"Yes, and she and I were too . . . but she's gone, okay? Anything else I can help you with?"

"Do you have an address?"

"Course I have a bloody address—and I'm not allowed within a hundred miles of it!"

He started to close the door. Eddie made the mistake of putting a foot out to stop him. It was the action of a braver, and much bigger, man. Mo's dad glared down at it in shock. Eddie glared down at it in shock. This was a man fresh out of prison. For shooting people. Eddie wanted to remove his foot straightaway. But it was frozen in place. His whole leg was frozen. And his brain.

"Can I . . . have the address?"

"No!"

"You . . . m-must be able . . . to tell me . . . something else . . . ," Eddie stammered.

"Something else?" shouted Mo's dad. "How about this? BUGGER OFF!"

He brought his foot down hard on Eddie's; Eddie let out a yelp and hopped backward onto the footpath. Mo's dad slammed the door.

Eddie crouched down on the pavement and massaged his foot. He didn't think anything was broken, but his pride was pretty badly dented.

Mo was gone.

Gone for good.

She was a silly, white-haired little girl, no use to anyone. But how on earth was he going to take over the world without her?

Two

The theft of the head of Oliver Plunkett was big news indeed. The Primate of All Ireland, the most important man in the Irish Church, rushed to St. Peter's in Drogheda the following morning and addressed a press conference from the steps outside. Television news crews, reporters and photographers jostled each other for the best view of the proceedings.

It is the wont of priests to speak in a rather convoluted fashion, whereas most people, particularly when they're sitting in pews listening to a service, just want them to get to the point. You don't stand up in church and shout, "Hey, Bishop, get to the bloody point"; but reporters, who believe not in God, but in their divine right to ask impertinent questions, do not usually show such restraint.

The primate had a deep, resonant voice, which sounded a bit like people imagine God himself to sound, if for instance they bumped into him while he was ordering a pizza. "Oliver Plunkett was a saint and a scholar," he was telling the reporters, "the last Catholic martyr in Britain. He was the first Irishman to become a saint in seven hundred years. As you know people travel from all over the world to ask for his blessing, to help cure their ills, to be inspired by . . ."

The reporters had had enough of this old guff. They wanted the facts.

"Do you have any idea who took the head?" one shouted.

The primate had no idea who had shouted the question, but glared in his general direction for a long moment, before clasping his hands and saying: "No." Realizing that this wasn't enough for them—because he'd be appearing on the lunchtime news later, and it was important to look as if he was in control of the situation—he quickly added: "The police are investigating, and I place great faith in their abilities. And great faith in the power of God to lead us to the culprits."

"How will this affect the pope's visit?" another reporter shouted.

"I hope to have the head returned safely before—"

Before he could finish, another question was hurled toward him.

"What about the head itself? Will it degenerate now that it has been removed from the special conditions it was kept in within the church?"

The primate shook his head. "There are no special conditions in the church. The head has been preserved by God's will, and so shall it be returned."

A female reporter raised her hand, and thankful for some politeness at last, the primate nodded at her.

"Is there not a legend that if the head is removed from the church a religious war will follow, leading to thousands of deaths and the collapse of civilization?"

"No."

The primate answered half a dozen more questions before calling a halt. He hurried back inside and down a long dark corridor to where other senior members of the church had gathered outside a small dark room which contained just a table and two chairs. It was like an interview room at a police station. And to all intents and purposes, it was. There was a small glass panel in the door through which the primate could see what was going on inside, and above it an air vent covered in wire mesh, which allowed him to hear what was being said. One voice, that belonging to Bishop Tuohey, didn't require an air vent; it was so loud, so frightening, that it could have been heard through several very thick walls; the other could barely be heard at all.

"The boy's name?" the primate asked.

Father Dougan, a small squat man, the primate's chief assistant, consulted a file in his hands. "Patrick Rice. Pat. Ten years old. Orphan from the Plunkett's home."

The primate studied the boy through the glass panel. "He looks younger. And he witnessed the theft?"

"So he says."

The primate nodded thoughtfully, then returned his

attention to the cross-examination taking place within. Pat was staring at the table, his arms folded, his legs not long enough to reach the floor; his face was red, his eyes were red rimmed; he'd thought he was doing the right thing by telling the headmaster about the theft. But now he realized that his mate Sean had been right. He should have kept his mouth shut. Bishop Tuohey was a huge, imposing figure who scared the pants off him. When he spoke he peppered Pat's face with flecks of spit. His voice was loud enough to burst eardrums.

"You stole into the church at night! You stole Oliver Plunkett's head!"

"No, Your Eminence!"

"You were in the church!"

"I just came to take a look."

"You just came and took the head!"

"I didn't! These men came in! They were wearing masks! They took the head!"

Pat jumped as Bishop Tuohey slammed his fist down on the table. "A big boy took it and ran away, is that it!"

"No . . . please . . . Your Eminence, I told you everything. I gave you their number. I gave you the license plates on their car . . ."

"You gave me *a* number, a makey-uppy number!"

"No!"

"Do you know what happens to boys who tell lies?"

"I'm not—"

"They burn in Hell for all eternity!"

Pat shut his eyes tight. Hell. He was going to Hell.

"I think that's enough, Bishop Tuohey."

Pat opened his eyes a fraction and saw that another man had entered the room, also dressed in the fine vestments of the church, but he looked somehow more powerful than the bishop.

"Primate? The boy's lying through his teeth. . . ."

The primate looked down at Pat, then shook his head slowly. "I don't think so." Pat sighed with relief. The primate turned back to the door and nodded at Father Dougan. Dougan immediately handed him a piece of paper, which the primate read. Then he glanced up at Bishop Tuohey.

"The number he gave us belongs to a car that was stolen in Belfast day before yesterday. What do you think the chances are of him making a number like that up?"

Tuohey nevertheless continued to glare down at Pat. "Doesn't mean he's not in it with them," he growled.

"I'm not, I swear to—"

Pat didn't finish. In some ways it was the perfectly obvious place in which to swear to God. But being surrounded by primates and bishops and priests, Pat decided it was probably better not to take the chance.

"Okay, Pat," the primate said, "you can leave us now. Although I'm sure the police would like a statement."

Pat, the sweat thick on his back, got cautiously up from his chair and began to follow the primate out of the room. He jumped suddenly as a sharp, bony finger was poked into his back. "If you'd come to us last night," Tuohey hissed, "we might have been able to stop them before they crossed the border."

"I'm sorry . . . ," Pat began. The bishop was horrible and scary, but he probably had a point.

"Don't give me your sorrys. You might as well have your filthy little fingers on it! Now get out of my sight, and don't come looking to me for absolution!"

Tuohey turned left outside the door to follow the primate and the other priests, while Father Dougan led Pat to the right, to where two police officers were waiting. As he approached them Pat saw Sean sitting on a chair, his arms folded, looking extremely angry. His left eye was swollen and bloodshot. He'd been smacked in the face, and it wasn't hard to guess who by.

"You little squealer," Sean hissed at him.

"I'm sorry . . . ," Pat said, "I was only trying to—"

He hadn't meant to use Sean's name, but Bishop Tuohey had been shouting so much and threatening him with so many punishments that it had seemed the only way to get him off his back. Sean had seen the car pull away as well. He'd seen the men take the head of Oliver Plunkett. Pat had had no alternative. But Sean obviously didn't see it that way.

"Soon as you're back in the home," said Sean, "we're gonna nail you to the wall. That's what we do to squealers."

Before Pat could respond the police led him away up the corridor to yet a different room. When he glanced back Sean was still glaring after him.

The second interview was much more straightforward. The cops were almost pleasant. They got him a can of Coke and a Twix. He told them his account of the night before, they asked him some questions, and when he was a bit vague with a reply they asked him for more detail. If Bishop Tuohey's line of questioning was like being savaged by a wolf, then this was like being in a pillow fight.

When it was over Pat had to hang around the church while the police called the orphanage to send down a teacher to pick him up. Sean had evidently already been returned. Doubtless he was now planning his revenge. Pat shuddered. The orphanage was not an easy place to live at the best of times, but at least in Sean he'd found a friend he could rely on. Now he'd not only lost an ally, but also probably gained the distrust and enmity of every boy in the home. Sean was right. Nobody likes a squealer.

Pat sighed. He would just have to accept his punishment.

That was what life was like.

Hard.

His parents, killed in a car crash.

His relatives didn't want to know.

Packed off to an orphanage, hardly old enough to tie his own shoelaces.

Smacked around the head on a daily basis, and that by the teachers.

Yet it was all he knew. It was home.

While he waited for the teacher to arrive, Pat wandered into the church. He looked up at the Virgin Mary. At the statues of the cross and the stained-glass depiction of events from the Gospels. All his life the importance of doing the right thing had been drilled into him, and now he had tried to do the right thing, and it had been thrown right back in his face. Bishop Tuohey had told him he was going to Hell, and Sean had promised to make his life Hell.

"Yeah," Pat said out loud, "thanks a bunch, God. Big help you are."

From somewhere behind him a deep voice said, "Saying something similar myself."

Pat turned slowly, terrified that God had somehow come down from Heaven to personally cut his tongue out for being cheeky.

It wasn't God. But it was pretty close. The primate, sitting half in shadow in the very back row of pews.

"I'm . . . s-sorry," Pat stammered, "I didn't mean to—"

"No, son," the primate said, standing now and coming fully into the light, "you're quite right. Sometimes it feels like he isn't listening at all. Sometimes it's his way of saying sort it out yourself, you're a big fella now."

Pat nodded awkwardly. The primate came up and patted his shoulder, then indicated for him to take a pew. Pat sat. The primate sat on the opposite side of the aisle, close enough to talk to Pat but far enough away not to intimidate him.

"I love this old church," the primate said, clasping his hands across his knees and rocking back to look up at the ceiling. "Came here when I was a boy. Your age. Didn't think I'd ever be a priest, never mind all this nonsense . . ." and he pulled at his vestments and shook his head.

Pat smiled. "What . . . ," he began, and then stopped. The primate raised an eyebrow, which Pat took as permission to continue. "What were *you* telling God off for?"

28

The primate nodded to himself for a moment. "Well now," he said, "I suppose, for getting me into this situation, and not showing me how to get out of it."

"You mean the head?"

"That's part of it, Pat. You see, son, you're only young, and to you it's just an old head in a glass case. But I have seen what it can do. I have seen a blind man cured. I have seen a lame man walk. I have seen tears fall from the dead eyes of Oliver Plunkett."

A shiver ran through Pat. He looked back up to the top of the church. The primate was saying that the head of Oliver Plunkett really could perform miracles—and yet Pat had stood up there and called him a coconut.

He was *definitely* going to Hell.

"You see, Pat, there's more to the church than just singing hymns and going to confession. We are God's representatives on earth. You know that His Holiness the pope is coming to Ireland?"

Pat nodded. Of course he knew. It seemed like every house in the country was flying yellow and white papal flags to mark the occasion; every window had a photograph of the pope in it.

"He's an old man now, his time is coming to an end. When he dies there will be a new pope, and the feeling is that he should come from Ireland. There hasn't been an Irish pope in a thousand years. It is our time, Pat. It is *my* time."

"You're going to be the next pope?"

The primate gave a little shrug. "There are those who would hope otherwise."

Pat wasn't sure what the primate was getting at. But he was feeling bold enough now to question him further. He was sitting with the most powerful priest in Ireland, and they were getting on like great mates. "What do you mean?" he asked.

"Ah, Pat. There are those who would covet the job themselves. Both within the Irish church and without. There are those who might think that stealing Oliver Plunkett's head days before the pope was due to visit it and bless it, well, that this was a way to embarrass me in front of him. And that's why I'm saying to God in here, thanks a bunch for letting me down on the home stretch. I thought all I had to do to become pope was to show up and sign on the dotted line. And now someone's gone and thrown a spanner in the works."

The primate let out a long sigh. Then he put his hands on the rail above the pews and pulled himself up. "Well," he said, "I should go. No rest for the wicked, eh, Pat?"

He reached across and tousled Pat's hair, then tramped slowly away up the aisle.

Pat sat for several minutes, thinking hard, all the while staring at the icons: at the Virgin Mary, at Jesus on the cross, at the empty space where Oliver Plunkett's head had once sat.

He had come into the church and told God off.

And now it seemed to him that God had come back with a pretty quick response, even quicker than e-mail. The primate hadn't spelled it out exactly, but it was quite clear what he was suggesting.

He was saying, Pat, the only way you're going to avoid

going to Hell is if you can get me the head back before the pope comes to visit.

Some people might argue that Pat was putting two and two together and getting twenty-seven.

But to Pat it was blindingly obvious.

He stood up.

He had made up his mind.

He would get the head back.

He would save the primate, and make sure he became pope.

He was on a mission.

A mission from God.

Three

Eddie was sitting watching TV with his bruised foot up on the sofa when he heard the key in the front door. He just had time to squash the box of Jaffa cakes he'd accidentally come across after a careful search of his mum's bedroom down the back of the cushions before she entered the apartment.

There were no *hello*s, or *how has your day been*s, she just tutted and said: "Why aren't you ready?"

"Ready for what?" Eddie snapped back.

She sighed. "Eddie. You've a head like a sieve."

"A what?"

"A sieve."

"Yes, I heard what you said, I just don't know what the hell you're talking about."

"Don't speak to me like that, Eddie."

"Then speak English. What's a sieve?"

She sighed again. "It's a kitchen utensil for draining the water from vegetables. It has lots of holes in it."

"What are you saying—that I'm a vegetable or I've got lots of holes in my head?"

"I'm not. Eddie, get your shoes on, we're going to be late."

"Late for what?"

"Eddie! For goodness' sake. I *told* you." She shook her head. "Eddie—take a wild guess. New city. New apartment. New . . . ?"

"PlayStation?"

"School, Eddie!"

Ah. Right. The penny dropped. Eddie glanced at his watch. "It's four o'clock. I think we've missed it for today."

"You're not funny, Eddie. The shops close in an hour, and you need a new uniform. So get your shoes on and let's get moving."

Eddie laughed. "Yeah. Right, Mum. Very funny. First of all, by the time we walk into the center of town, the shops will be closed. Second of all, we don't even know what school I'm going to yet. And third of all, we've an entire week until the schools go back, so what's the hurry?"

Eddie's mum was not amused, but that didn't worry Eddie. He knew parents got frustrated and upset when they realized they were stupider than their children. Eddie flicked channels.

"Eddie!"

"What?"

She began to count off on her fingers. "Number one—

we're not walking into town, Bernard has the car outside! Number two—we do know what school you're going to—Brown's Academy! And number three—it's the best school in Belfast, and it starts back a week before every other school. And that's tomorrow! So get your trainers on and get out here *now*!"

She spun on her heel and stormed back out of the apartment.

Eddie sat stunned.

Talk about information overload.

He didn't know whether to laugh, scream, cry, shout or curl up in a ball and die. What had she said? Eddie sat where he was and attempted to analyze his mother's explosion of information in a calm and collected manner.

First of all—*Bernard*'s car? Bernard could only be Bernard J. Scuttles, head of security at the hospital, and the man who'd been sworn to stay away from his mum as a condition of his being rescued from the baby-snatchers. Bernard who hated Eddie with a vengeance. Bernard who was married to someone else. Bernard who wanted to sleep in the same bed as Eddie's mum. Bernard whom his mum had sworn not to see again after she'd found out he was married. Bernard the slimeball. Bernard the bully. Bernard the . . .

Okay—enough, enough.

Next point—Brown's Academy.

"Eddie!" his mum screamed from the hall.

"Just putting my shoes on!"

Brown's Academy—what on earth was Brown's Academy? Eddie knew that there were two secondary schools relatively close at hand—and more importantly he'd worked out how to get to each of them without passing through Reservoir Pups territory, so he'd been fairly relaxed about going to either of them. But Brown's Academy? He'd never heard of it. It certainly wasn't within walking distance like the others.

And as for going back to school one week before every other kid in the city—what sort of lunatics were they? It was still the summer. It was still August, for God's sake. How could you go back to school in August? Were all the pupils, not to mention the teachers, so dumb that they needed an extra week's work? Was he going to a school designed for boys with heads like drained vegetables, or whatever the hell it was Mum had been talking about?

"EDDIE!"

"Coming!"

Eddie rolled off the couch and picked up his loose trainer.

He had a bad feeling about this. Eddie's bad feelings were usually spot on.

It is said that there are only two types of people: those who describe, for example, a glass of Sunny Delight as being half empty, and those who describe it as being half full. Those who look at the dark side—i.e., I've nearly finished my drink and I don't know where the next one is going to come from. And those who look at the bright side—i.e., I really enjoyed that drink, there's still half a glass left and there's probably more in the fridge. A pessimist, who thinks there's no hope, and an optimist, who looks forward to the future and smiles a lot. But Eddie made a pessimist look like an optimist. Because no matter how gloomy a pessimist was, Eddie knew from sad personal experience that things were probably going to turn out even worse than he could imagine. That the glass was not only clearly half empty, but that what was left in it was probably full of poison.

Eddie's mum on the other hand could look at the glass and say, "Why, that's a lovely glass, I wonder where I could buy five more to match it?"

But then she was a headcase, as you would have to be to even contemplate kissing Bernard J. Scuttles, as Eddie had discovered her doing on more than one occasion. Eddie didn't even want to climb into the same car as him. Scuttles made Eddie sick. In fact he could probably force himself to actually be sick all over Scuttles' backseat just to teach him a lesson. Right down behind the cushions where it would be impossible to clean it up; he could be sick in the ashtrays and the glove compartment. He could be sick into the heater, so that as soon as Scuttles switched it on it would spray everyone in the car with hot vomit. He could . . .

"Hello, Eddie," Scuttles said as Eddie climbed into the car.

"Hello, Fat Chops," said Eddie.

Scuttles' mouth curled up into a snarl, but before he could say anything Eddie's mum slipped into the front seat, and he thought better of it.

Because he's sneaky, Eddie thought.

Because he wants to kiss her later.

Bernard smiled at his mum, and then smiled back at Eddie. "So, Eddie, have you enjoyed your summer holidays?"

"Yeah, great," said Eddie. "How's your wife?"

Scuttles looked stunned, but recovered quickly and was on the verge of snapping something back when Eddie's mum put a restraining hand on his leg.

She's touching his big fat hairy leg! Ughhhhhhhh!

Scuttles took a deep breath, then forced a smile onto his face. "For your information, Eddie," he said, "my wife and I are getting a divorce. Now there's nothing to stop us being together." He leaned over and kissed Eddie's mum on the cheek. She flushed a little and smiled shyly back at her son. Eddie slumped back in his seat.

Great.

Swell.

Fantastic.

It was time to change the subject. "So what on earth is Brown's Academy?"

Scuttles glanced back at him. "School for snobs," he said.

"Oh don't, Bernard," his mum reprimanded lightly, "it's not like that. Brown's Academy is a private school, Eddie, it costs a small fortune, but it has the best reputation in the whole city. Boys who go there go on to become surgeons, and scientists and government ministers."

"A *private* school?" Eddie asked. His heart wasn't sinking. It had sunk. "You mean all the little rich kids? All the spoilt little brats? And you're *paying* for it? I don't think so."

"Eddie, it's not as if you have a choice."

"Oh, I think I do."

"Oh, I think you don't. Eddie, all I want is the best for you, and I've scrimped and saved to send you to Brown's, so that's where you're going."

"And I appreciate all of your effort, but why don't you keep the money, buy yourself a nice dress and send me to St. Coleman's, it's just round the corner, or Orangefield, it's just down the road."

"You're going to Brown's."

"But I don't want to go there. And not that it matters, but where is it, anyway?"

"It's in the south of the city. Just a couple of stops on the train."

"The *train*?" Eddie shouted. "What on earth do I want to get a train for? I can walk to the other schools in five minutes."

His mum turned more fully in the seat now and looked gravely at him. "Eddie, you might be able to walk to them, but it doesn't mean they'll let you in."

"And what's that supposed to mean?"

His mum sighed. She glanced at Scuttles, then back at him. "Eddie, to tell you the truth I would have been quite happy to let you go to St. Coleman's. Or to Orangefield. But the simple fact of the matter is that neither of them want you."

"What are you talking about? You mean they don't think I'm smart enough? I've met boys from those schools—and they're morons."

Scuttles snorted, "Tell him, darlin', tell him the truth."

Eddie's mum shook her head. Scuttles wagged a finger back at him. "Eddie, it's not that you're not smart enough. It's because you're a troublemaker."

"A WHAT?"

"Their words, Eddie, not mine. All that stuff about you breaking into the hospital and the babies being stolen, well they just said they could do without that kind of a boy."

"But I saved the babies! I'm a hero!"

"In your own head," said Scuttles.

His mum smiled sympathetically back at him. "Well, that's not how they look at it, they think you're a law unto yourself. And . . . well, you have to admit they might have a point."

"That's not fair!"

"Well, that's how it is. And the truth of the matter is that Brown's is the only school that would take you and that only because they're desperate for money. It's costing me a fortune. So you'll go there and you'll enjoy it. There, I've said it."

"I will not!"

"Yes you will!"

"Will not!"

"Either that or the Social Services will take you away and put you in a home."

"Rather that than go to bloody Brown's. They'll all be stuck-up little poofs."

"Well," said Scuttles, "you'll fit in perfectly."

The shop which sold the uniforms for Brown's Academy was five minutes from closing when they arrived, and they didn't look too happy when Scuttles opened the door for Eddie's mum, who dragged Eddie in by the ear.

Well, not quite by the ear.

A metaphorical ear, which is like a real ear, only invisible and much bigger and probably more painful when pulled mercilessly by a cruel mum who sends her only son to a horrendous school.

But he was fuming.

He had saved twelve babies, he'd been given reward money and been hailed as a hero. And now he was being treated like he was the villain, like he'd stolen the babies. Life just was not fair. His glass was not only half empty, it was completely empty, and somebody had smashed it and stuck jagged pieces of glass into his bum.

The man who owned the shop was tall and as thin as a rake. He looked like a giraffe with glasses. He'd been supplying uniforms for so long that he didn't even have to measure Eddie for size, he just gave him the briefest glance and then disappeared into a storeroom to find a blazer.

Eddie sat and stared at the floor.

Mum tousled his hair and said, "Don't worry, love, it'll be fine. You'll love it."

Eddie grunted.

She went to look at shirts.

Scuttles came closer and reached out a hand, as if to tousle his hair as well.

"If you touch my hair," Eddie snapped, "I'll break off your fingers and stick them up your nose."

"I wasn't going to," Scuttles shot back, then nipped Eddie on the cheek.

Eddie let out a yelp and kicked out at Scuttles, but he'd already danced out of range, laughing.

Then the giraffe brought back the blazer.

It was purple.

Bright purple.

He held it up proudly. Eddie's mum went, "Awww, isn't it lovely?"

Eddie's mouth was hanging open.

Even Scuttles looked a little distressed. "Is it a girls' school he's going to?" he asked.

The giraffe was deeply offended by this. "No, it is *not* a girls' school. These have been the colors of Brown's Academy for one hundred and seventy-five years."

"Well, they've had crap taste for one hundred and seventy-five years," Eddie observed.

"Eddie!" his mum snapped.

The giraffe looked down his nose at Eddie. "If the young master would feel happier at a less prestigious establishment, then I'm sure—"

Eddie's mum cut in. "No . . . no . . . he doesn't mean anything. . . ." She smiled endearingly at the giraffe. "He's just at that awkward age," she said, and winked.

The giraffe gave Eddie a dismissive look and turned toward the cash register. "If you ask me," he said, "they always are."

Eddie very rarely agreed with anything Scuttles had to say, but this time he had to admit he had a point.

The blazer.

It would make him look like a girl.

And now, he realized, to get to the train, to take him to Brown's, he would have to pass through Reservoir Pups territory.

Dressed like a girl.

Eddie gave a sigh of utter despair.

The giraffe said, "That'll be ninety pounds, ma'am."

His mum turned to Scuttles. "Bernard, your checkbook."

It was Bernard's turn to look shocked. "M-my . . . what?" he stammered.

"You will learn, Bernard," Eddie's mum said gravely, "that there is no such thing as a free kiss. You do want a kiss, don't you?"

Bernard took a deep breath, then nodded at Eddie's mum and reached for his checkbook.

Four

Pat planned to escape from the St. Oliver Plunkett orphanage at midnight. No particular reason for midnight—just seemed like the kind of time when people normally escaped from places. He had packed his few belongings together in a small, battered rucksack but kept it out of sight in the locker by his bed. He checked his watch. It was now a little before eleven, and the lights in the dormitory had been out for an hour. He listened as the whispers in the dark began to die down, as the steady rhythm of sleep fell over his fellow orphans. He was tired and could easily have slept himself but he didn't dare close his eyes, partly because he knew that if he fell into a deep sleep he would lose his best chance to escape, but mostly because he was scared of the nightmares that were bound to come. Pat always had bad dreams, about the home usually and being beaten with sticks by the teachers—which had never happened, thankfully—or about his parents, their skeletal hands reaching out to him, trying to pull him into their graves. But tonight if he fell asleep he knew he would dream about Bishop Tuohey and eternal damnation and Hell and wake up screaming, which would not help his escape plan much.

So Pat lay in the dark, glancing at his watch every five minutes to check the time. It was digital, but it was about thirty years old, a big clumpy thing some Creep had given to him at Christmas. That was what the boys called them—Creeps. Grown-ups who came to the orphanage at Christmas because they felt guilty about the wonderful life they had and it made them feel better to present gifts to the poor little children who had no parents. Except instead of going out and buying them shiny, new, modern gifts they brought presents which they had received themselves but didn't want, the embarrassing sweaters, the awful CDs, the watches which hadn't been fashionable since Noah built his ark. Real, proper, modern digital watches—you could send e-mail, could find out the time in New York, they could almost make you a cup of coffee. This one just told you the time, nothing else—the fractured numbers glowing red in the dark. It didn't emit much light—but just enough to see . . .

Figures moving in the darkness.

Pat wasn't sure if he was imagining things at first, whether his eyes were playing tricks on him. But no, there was definitely movement, and sound as well—bedsprings squeaking, the bare floorboards creaking, conspiratorial whispers. He blinked his eyes, wondering if he was imagining it, or if he had fallen asleep and was dreaming.

But then suddenly he was under attack and he knew this was no dream.

It was a nightmare, but a living, breathing, real nightmare. Fists were raining down on him; feet were plowing into him.

It felt as if every boy in the dorm was attacking him.

It felt that way because it was true.

They were all beating him up.

Pat hid as best he could under the blankets, but they provided little protection. He curled himself up like a hedgehog, but the fists found their way through; when he hugged his head, they pounded his stomach; when he moved to protect his stomach, they pounded his head.

The only good thing—and it was a very, very, very, very, very small good thing—was that there were so many boys wanting to attack him that they were getting in each other's way; some of the punches were missing; some of the kicks were striking other boys instead of the intended target, so that instead of being struck five hundred times, he only actually got struck three hundred and twenty-seven times.

Easy, really.

He could have screamed for help, but he didn't make a sound.

Even though they could easily have beaten him to death, he didn't call on the teachers or the priests who ran the home because he knew that if he lived through the night, crying like a baby and calling for help would only make things worse for him.

He had betrayed Sean's trust, and this was the punishment.

He would just have to grin and bear it.

Although he would have to grin through broken teeth.

The attack seemed to last for about an hour, but it could only have been a couple of minutes. In the darkness somebody said, "Enough," and then they slipped back to their beds; in a matter of seconds an almost perfect calm had returned to the dorm, as if nothing had even happened; the only sound Pat could hear was that of a boy whimpering in the darkness, like a dog who'd been beaten; and the sound was coming from him.

Pat finally slipped out of the home about an hour before dawn. His arms and legs were stiff and sore from the beating and one of his front teeth was missing and another was decidedly wobbly, but otherwise he was remarkably well considering that twenty boys had tried to play football with his skull. He dropped down over the wall, then looked back up at the home, in darkness but for a light by the front door. He had lived there for six years. The boys came and the boys went, but he was always there. It was home, and he felt somehow sad to be leaving it. But it had to be done. He had to find the head of Oliver Plunkett.

First stop was Drogheda Station to catch the Belfast train. It was only a short walk from the home. Although the car park outside it was already dotted with cars, the main station building itself was not yet open. But he wasn't going to bother with the main building for the simple reason that he wasn't going to bother with a train ticket; he had the grand total of three euros in his pocket; it was hardly enough for a Coke and a Twix.

Pat skirted the car park and then moved down a boundary wall until all that was dividing him from the rail track was a wire fence. He was over that in a minute. Then he crouched down behind some oil drums to wait: he didn't know which would arrive first, the train for Belfast, or daylight.

After about half an hour of crouching, shivering in the darkness, lights came on in the station, and shortly afterward passengers began to congregate on the platform. Ten minutes later Pat saw lights along the line and the Belfast Express slowly pulled past him; it was already crowded with passengers traveling from Dublin; he could see them reading their newspapers, or drinking their coffee or, mostly, with their heads resting against the windows, trying to sleep. Pat slipped out from his hiding place and joined the crush of people trying to get on board.

Once inside Pat passed through the first class carriage and continued on toward the back of the train. He found a seat two carriages from the end; there was a woman sitting opposite reading a newspaper. The story on the front was about the theft of the head. There was no photograph of Oliver Plunkett's head—but there was an artist's impression of what it looked like. Pat guessed this was because the paper wanted to make the head appear more mysterious and miraculous than it really was. There was still no getting away from the fact that old Ollie looked like a coconut in real life, or death, as the case may be.

But this drawing on the front of the newspaper made him look—well, *recently* dead. He still had flesh, his hair looked freshly washed, and his eyes: well, his eyes seemed to be staring directly at Pat.

Even when Pat moved seats, from beside the aisle to right up close against the window, when he glanced back at the paper Oliver Plunkett's dead eyes were still staring at him. Pat shuddered. He closed his own eyes. He rested his head against the window. Within a few minutes the steady rhythm of the train as it glided across the tracks had sent him to sleep.

"Tickets, please."
Pat was lost in a dream of Hell. A nightmare. A daymare.
"Tickets, please."
There was a huge horn-headed monster coming toward him.
"Tickets, please."
There were flames and steam and people screaming.
"TICKETS, PLEASE!"
A horrible scaly hand was reaching out to . . .
"TICKETS, PLEASE!!!!!"

Pat opened his eyes. He was bathed in sweat. The train's conductor, a portly man with three chins, was standing in the aisle glaring in at Pat and . . . the woman opposite him had evidently got off at some point. There was now a scruffy-looking man in a crumpled suit lying slumped against the window, snoring.

"Are you deaf or stupid?" the conductor inquired.

"I-I'm . . . ," Pat stammered. There was probably just enough space to squeeze past the conductor and run for it—but run where? He was a prisoner on the train. And the conductor was big enough to swat him like a fly, and then sit on him until they got to Belfast. Then he'd be handed over to the police and sent back to the orphanage, where he'd be beaten up for running away by the teachers instead of the boys. "I'm . . . with my da," Pat said, and pointed across at the sleeping man.

"Well, wake him up, I need your tickets."

"I can't," said Pat, "he's exhausted."

"Just give him a poke," said the conductor.

"I can't. He'll whack me if I wake him."

The conductor let out a sigh, then came forward himself to give the man a nudge.

"No . . . no, wait," said Pat. "Let me."

Pat moved off his seat and approached the snoring man. He cautiously lifted back one side of his jacket and reached into his inside pocket. It was empty. The other side of his jacket was pinned down by an arm. Pat took a deep breath, then carefully took a light hold of the arm and slowly moved it to one side, freeing that side of the jacket. The man muttered something in his sleep, then readjusted his position. Thankfully his arm stayed where it was. Pat reached inside his other pocket and removed the man's wallet. He flipped it open. There was about two hundred euros inside.

"We didn't have time to get tickets," said Pat. "Can we buy two?"

"Course you can," said the conductor. Pat gave him

fifty euros and the man duly presented him with two tickets and some change. He even winked at Pat and said, "You make a grand little thief," and turned away. Pat smiled to himself. He looked down at the wallet. At the rest of the euros. Over a hundred and fifty left. He could probably live quite comfortably on a hundred and fifty euros. At least until he got the head back.

But no. He was on a mission from God.

He couldn't go around stealing people's wallets.

He had bought the tickets out of desperation.

God would understand that.

But he certainly wouldn't understand stealing the other hundred and fifty as well.

Pat hesitated.

He would need *some* money.

After all, he wouldn't be able to reclaim the head if he starved to death.

He had to eat. He had to put his head down somewhere.

He would keep fifty euros.

No, a hundred.

What was a hundred euros compared to getting back the revered head of Oliver Plunkett?

What was a hundred euros compared to the Primate of All Ireland becoming the next pope?

For that matter, what was a hundred and fifty euros?

He wasn't stealing it. He was borrowing it forever.

The man wasn't losing a hundred and fifty euros, he was investing it in the Church.

That was it, it was an investment.

Satisfied that he was no longer a thief, more of a religious stockbroker, Pat turned to slip the now empty wallet back into the snoring man's jacket.

Except that he was no longer snoring. He was sitting with his arms folded, coolly watching Pat.

"He's right," the man said, "you are a grand little thief." He reached forward, grabbed Pat's jacket, and pulled him close. "Now give me back my money," he growled.

Five

"But why can't I get a taxi?" said Eddie, halfway out of the door on his way to his first morning at Brown's Academy.

"Who do you think you are, Prince Charles?" said his mother. "Because it would cost a fortune—and it's costing me enough to send you to Brown's, never mind a taxi. We're not made of money, you know."

Eddie was wearing his bright purple blazer.

He looked like an idiot.

A big girl idiot.

His mother gently pushed him out of the door and in so doing attempted to kiss the top of his head, but he successfully squirmed out of the way. He fumed on the way down in the lift, he fumed as he crossed the car park and he fumed as he stood in the entrance to the nurses' home grounds deciding what to do. To his left was the Royal Victoria Hospital, to his right the road leading to the huge and sprawling Rivers Estate, the headquarters of the Reservoir Pups, the most feared gang in the city. Straight ahead of him was a roundabout, which was circled by the motorway, and beyond that was Sandy Row, another sprawling mass of houses which Eddie would have to walk through to get to Botanic Station. This would have been dangerous enough a few weeks previously, because the Sandy Row Revengers were a small but violent gang who demanded payment from any kids passing through their territory, but Eddie knew for a fact that the Revengers had since been attacked and defeated by the Pups and were no longer in control of their own territory. It was clear to him that the Pups, flush with money and power, were intent on expanding their empire. And that was not good news for Eddie.

He stared across the road toward Sandy Row. He tried to work out if he really had any alternative: it was now just before 8 a.m., and it would take him a good twenty minutes to walk to the station if he went through Sandy Row. Then there'd be another twenty minutes on the train. He'd arrive at Brown's Academy just in time to find his way around in time for a 9 a.m. start. But if he went any other way: it would take him at least an hour to walk around the outside of Sandy Row, he'd miss his train, he'd miss the start of school, and how good was that going to look, both to the school and to his mum, who was paying so much to send him there?

Eddie sighed. He wanted to run away. He wanted to

call his dad and say, hey, Dad, help me out here, but he had no dad. Not anymore. He'd taken off to England without a word. Not one. Eddie was starting to hate his dad. A few weeks to get settled into his new life, that was what he'd allowed him. But there'd been nothing. Not a phone call, not a letter, not a huge present just to make him feel better. Nothing.

Eddie took off his blazer and folded it into his schoolbag. Walking through Sandy Row would be difficult enough without wearing a bright purple blazer. That left him wearing gray trousers, black shoes, a white shirt and a purple tie. Eddie took the tie off as well, and unbuttoned his top shirt button. There. He didn't look so bad. He still looked odd—but at least he didn't look like a girl.

Okay—here goes.

Eddie dodged the traffic on both sides of the roundabout, and nervously stepped into the tangled red-brick streets of Sandy Row. He walked at a steady pace—but didn't march. He kept his eyes either on the ground or straight ahead; when somebody passed him, adult or child, he didn't look in their direction, but neither did he look obviously away. He looked slightly to the side, or slightly above or below them. He worked his mouth so that it looked like he was chewing gum; he thought that might make him look a little bit tough, though in truth it made him look like a cow chewing its cud. Like he was devouring himself. After ten minutes he reckoned he was more than halfway toward the station; he'd seen some kids, but nobody had come near him. Perhaps it was going to be okay: most of the other gang members would still be off school, what reason did they have to be up at eight in the morning? They were still lying in their beds. On the other hand, he knew that the Reservoir Pups were a twenty-four-hour operation and were unlikely to leave their territory unguarded. So where were they?

Eddie's shirt was sticking to his back: not with the effort of walking, but with the stress of traversing such dangerous territory. His brain was sweating.

He kept walking.

After another five minutes he began to make out, in the distance the red *NIR* lettering on the front of Botanic Station.

The end was in sight.

This is the point, he thought, *this is the point where it all goes wrong.* That was what his life was like. *Good, luck* and *Eddie* were three words that were rarely heard in the same sentence. *This is where ten thousand Reservoir Pups storm out of a side street and dance on my head. This is where I step on a land mine. This is where a huge piano falls out of the sky and crushes me.*

But he walked on.

And on.

And on.

And soon there was only a main road between him and the station; and here and there across the road, in amongst the men and women hurrying to catch their morning train, he could see other purple blazers, other boys going in the same direction as he was.

He had made it! Eddie stepped out onto the road.

"HEY!"

He froze. A voice from behind him. He didn't dare turn. He looked desperately to his left and right. The traffic was just too heavy for him to dart across.

"HEY, EDDIE!"

The voice was familiar.

It was them. They'd found him. They'd given him a glimpse of victory, and now they were going to snatch it away from him. . . .

"Eddie—wait!"

It was so much closer now. One voice. Just one. He could turn, punch the owner of the voice and still make it across the road. Eddie bunched his hands into fists. This was it, he was going to make a fight of it. He wasn't scared of the Reservoir Pups. No—wait, that wasn't right. He was scared of them. He was terrified of them. But he kept his fists ready. Okay, so he was terrified. But men who fought wars were terrified. Men who climbed mountains were terrified. Sometimes that was what made them great, being terrified, and facing up to it.

So Eddie faced up to it.

He turned, ready to fight.

And the lollipop man said: "You shouldn't cross without me, you know."

Eddie stared at him. And around him, looking for the Pups. But no, it was only the lollipop man.

"Oh—right—s-sorry," Eddie stammered and took a step back onto the footpath. He waited for the lollipop man to step out and stop the oncoming cars, feeling rather foolish that he'd been frightened so easily. And then he realized that the lollipop man wasn't making any effort to stop the traffic. And on top of that he realized that the lollipop man had called him Eddie.

Eddie turned quickly. The lollipop man was a large, unfit kind of a big lump in a white coat and white peaked cap. He was also carrying a large metal lollipop. "How . . . how do you know my name?" Eddie asked.

The lollipop man looked puzzled for a moment, and then, apparently realizing something, quickly smiled and removed his cap.

"Sorry, Eddie—last time you saw me I was—"

"Washing dead bodies! Barney!"

Barney was over six feet tall, a big, big man. Eddie had stumbled across him while being chased by the baby-snatchers through the Royal Victoria Hospital. He'd taken refuge in the room where the hospital kept its dead bodies before they were shipped off to funeral homes. It was Barney's job to wash them. It was, apparently, a job he really liked. When he'd discovered Eddie hiding amongst the bodies he could easily have turned him in, but instead had protected him.

"Hiya, Eddie, didn't expect to see you here."

"Barney—I'm going to school. But what are *you* doing here?"

"Didn't you hear? I got sacked from the hospital."

"Sacked? But why?"

"Your friend Scuttles got me sacked. Because I helped you escape."

"Scuttles! But . . . Barney, if you hadn't helped me I never would have rescued the babies."

Barney nodded sadly. "I know. But Scuttles said that at the time I didn't know that, that at the time I was helping a burglar to escape. So he got me sacked."

Eddie blew air out of his cheeks. "God, I hate that man," he said.

"You and me both," Barney said sadly. "I liked my job. I was good at my job. I made dead people smell good."

Eddie didn't particularly want to think about that, but he knew where Barney was coming from.

"Still," Barney said, suddenly brighter, a smile forced back onto his face, "I like this job too. It's me versus the drivers, and I always win!"

With that he stepped out onto the road with his lollipop, causing several cars to brake suddenly. Barney ignored their screaming horns, and ushered Eddie quickly across the road.

"Have a good day, Eddie!" he shouted after him. "See you tomorrow!"

Despite Eddie's anger with Scuttles, he couldn't help smiling to himself as he bought his train ticket and then walked down the ramp toward the platform. Barney was a little on the simple side, he thought, but his heart was in the right place. And he was just about the only friend Eddie had in the entire city.

He took a seat, then glanced around him. In amongst the workers he could see ten or twenty other boys in their purple blazers. Now that he could see so many of them, he thought that perhaps they weren't quite as girly as he had imagined. More . . . distinctive. Unique. Brave, even. As if they were saying, we know we look stupid—but we don't care. Eddie fished his tie out of his bag, put it on, then pulled out his blazer, flattened out the creases as best he could and pulled it on. Yeah. It didn't feel too bad.

When the train pulled in five minutes later Eddie found a seat near the front. There were other boys from Brown's sitting further back, but he chose not to sit beside them. There was no point in forcing himself on anyone. He would get to school, check out the lie of the land, see what his class was like. No point in making friends with anyone until he knew exactly what the situation was. He'd hold back. Be cool. And then he would start recruiting. Because if he was prevented from building up his gang at home, there was certainly nothing to stop him building one up in school. And if the other boys in his class came from rich backgrounds, then they'd have money to spend; and they'd probably look up to him because he came from a rough, tough area. Plus he was a hero. And if they didn't know he was a hero, well, he just happened to have some of the articles written in the newspaper about him in his schoolbag. How could they fail to be impressed?

Eddie felt good. He examined his reflection in the window. He didn't look round when somebody sat down beside him. He was too busy admiring himself and thinking about his plans for world domination. But he did look round when that somebody elbowed him in the ribs and said, "Love the uniform, Curly—you going to a girls' school?"

The voice was familiar—and unlike with Barney, he knew exactly who it was before he turned, clutching his ribs and stifling a shout of pain.

Bacon.

The first Reservoir Pup he'd ever met, the Pup who'd kidnapped him and taken him to Reservoir Pups headquarters. The Pup who in some respects was responsible for all his misfortunes.

And where Bacon was, his friend Bap was never far behind.

Or, in fact, *directly* behind.

Bap slapped his ear, hard; Eddie winced and ducked away.

When he eventually sat up again, pressing himself back against the window, he looked at their two grinning faces and said with as much bravado as he could manage:

"What the hell do you two want?"

Bacon pretended to be upset. "What kind of a way is that to greet an old friend?"

Eddie could have said, better than elbowing them in the ribs or smacking their ear. But he didn't. He said: "What do you want?"

Bap shook his head and said, "We just want to be friends, Eddie."

Eddie looked from one to the other. "Yeah—sure," he said.

"Enjoy your walk this morning?" Bacon asked.

"What?"

"Your walk through Sandy Row. You looked kind of nervous."

"I wasn't nervous."

"Well, you never waved at us once, and we were right behind you."

"You were not," said Eddie.

"Sure we were," said Bap. "Saw you talking to that big fat eejit used to work in the hospital. What you want to talk to a big tube like that for?"

"He's not a tube," said Eddie.

Bacon and Bap smiled at each other. Then Bacon poked Eddie with a finger. "The reason you weren't jumped in Sandy Row," he said, "was because Captain Black has a job for you."

Eddie looked incredulously from one to the other. "Wise up," he said.

"We're serious," said Bacon, "and you'd better take it serious."

Eddie pretended to laugh—although it was the least funny situation he'd been in for a long time. Captain Black, as leader of the Reservoir Pups, was his mortal enemy. He might be confined to a wheelchair, but he was still the most dangerous gang leader in the city. "Captain Black—sure, aren't we just best buddies."

"It's not about being buddies," Bap snapped, "it's about doing what you're told."

"And why would I even think for one minute about doing anything Captain Black says?"

Bacon gave a sad shake of his head. "Because, Curly—"

"My name's not Curly."

"Your name's what we say it is—Girly."

"Ah, act your age," said Eddie, without thinking.

Bacon grabbed his blazer and banged Eddie against the train window. Bap pulled his hair.

"You listen to me, Girly," Bacon shouted, "this is important. You do what Captain Black asks, or we will make your life a complete and utter misery."

Bap yanked his hair again. "You have to get to this train every morning. And every morning we're going to make sure you get a good kicking—unless you follow orders. You do what we say, you get safe passage. Understood?"

Eddie nodded warily.

"Good." Bap reached inside his jacket and withdrew an envelope. "In here," he said, flapping the envelope in Eddie's face, "is the name of a boy in your school. You're to make friends with him. Talk to him. We want a record kept of everything he says to you, do you understand?"

Eddie nodded again. "But . . . why? Who . . . is he?"

"His name's in the envelope."

"I don't mean his name, I mean—"

Bap yanked his hair again. "Just do what you're bloody told, Curly."

"We'll talk to you later."

With that Bacon and Bap got up from their seats. The train was just pulling into the next stop, the one before Eddie had to get off. Eddie breathed a sigh of relief. But then as Bacon and Bap waited for the doors to open a thought struck him and he shouted after them:

"But how did you know I was even going to Brown's Academy?"

Bap laughed as he stepped off. Bacon scowled back and said: "How did we know? We didn't *know*. We arranged it.

Captain Black made sure. All right, Curly? See you later."

And with that they both stepped off the train.

Eddie slumped back in his seat.

Everything changes, and everything remains the same.

Once again he'd been given a mission by the Reservoir Pups.

Once again he was at their mercy.

Great.

Just bloody great.

Six

So Pat gave the crumpled man in the crumpled suit his money back, except of course for what he'd already spent on his train tickets. The man scowled at him as he squashed the euros untidily into his wallet and then slipped it inside his jacket. He sat back then and folded his arms and said, "So, give me one good reason why I shouldn't get the police to arrest you."

Pat did what all boys of his age do, whether they're smart or stupid, when caught red-handed: he shrugged.

This, clearly, did not impress Crumples. He said, "That's not good enough, son."

Pat shrugged again.

Crumples said, "How old are you anyway? What're you doing on a train by yourself, this time of the morning?"

Pat shrugged.

"I know you can talk, because you talked to the conductor, so you can talk to me or I'll shop you to the police. I'm serious."

Pat shrugged again.

Crumples felt his outside jacket pockets, then produced a mobile phone. This time *he* shrugged, then said. "Please yourself." He punched in three numbers, waited for a moment then said: "Is that the police?"

"I'm on a mission from God," Pat said quickly.

"You're what?" said Crumples.

"I'm on a mission from God. I'm going to find the head of Oliver Plunkett."

Crumples' eyes narrowed. He spoke quickly into the phone. "I've just found my cat. Sorry to trouble you." He cut the line. "Tell me that again," he said to Pat.

"I'm going to find the head of Oliver Plunkett."

"And why would you want to find the head of Oliver Plunkett? And why would you be going to Belfast to do it?"

"Because I saw who took it, and I know where they're from."

Pat could almost see a light switching on in Crumples' eyes. His cheeks flushed, his demeanor softened, his whole body language changed. He was no longer the angry victim of a crime. He was Pat's friend. Or wanted to be.

"Why," he said, unfolding his arms and leaning forward, "it's wonderful that you would do such a thing."

Pat reverted to shrugging. He'd probably said too much already.

"Please," Crumples said, "tell me more."

"Nothing more to say," said Pat.

"But there must be," said Crumples. "Young fella like you, traveling to a different country, without adult supervision, without any money—and you say you saw the robbery? What did they look like?"

Pat shrugged.

"And how do you know they're from Belfast?"

Pat shrugged.

Crumples realized he wasn't getting anywhere. So he raised his phone again. "One call, it's all it takes."

Pat thought about this. He had revealed his mission out of desperation—because he knew if he was arrested by the police they'd either throw him in a cell or send him straight back to the orphanage, but now that he was being threatened with the police for a second time, it suddenly didn't seem quite so intimidating. Crumples seemed just a little too eager to find out what he was up to. If he was just an ordinary passenger who'd had his money stolen, why would he show so much interest in what Pat was up to? Why was he, in effect, blackmailing him for information about what he'd seen during the theft?

Crumples waved the phone at him again and raised an eyebrow.

Pat shrugged again, then looked out of the window. He was going to call Crumples' bluff.

Crumples dialed again. "Hello, is that the police?" He paused, then looked across at Pat. Pat could tell he was looking at him because he could see Crumples' reflection in the window. "Yes, I'd like to report a . . ." and then he paused, waiting for Pat to turn and plead with him; but Pat kept his eyes on the countryside flashing past outside. "I'd like to report . . . ," Crumples said again, hesitated, then said quickly, ". . . that my cat has come back again . . . I'm sorry to trouble you."

He cut the line again. Pat could hardly keep the smirk off his face.

Crumples nodded across at him. "All right, kid, have it your way." He reached into his jacket again, removed his wallet, flipped it open and removed a card. He handed it across to Pat. "You can read, can't you?" he said.

Pat took the card: it said, *Jack Matchitt, Reporter, Belfast Telegraph.* He went to hand it back, but Crumples—he much preferred thinking of him as Crumples rather than Jack Matchitt—held up his hand. "Keep it. You never know when you might need it."

"Why would I need it?" asked Pat.

"Well, son, you're on a mission from God. But God doesn't always answer the phone. I do."

Pat nodded for several moments, like he understood what Crumples was talking about, but then gave in and said, "What's that supposed to mean?"

"It means you scratch my back, I'll scratch yours."

"That doesn't help me much either."

Crumples gave him a look like he was stupid, sighed, then moved over to sit beside him. Pat instinctively moved further away. "Look, kid, if you're telling the truth, then you're a witness to a major crime, you have evidence about that crime that hasn't been released by the police.

You're a story. What do you think I'm doing on this train? I was down there yesterday for the Cardinal's press conference. They didn't tell us anything about there being a witness or that there was a Belfast connection. That's big news. And even bigger is some snotty-nosed kid setting out to get the head back."

"I don't have a snotty nose," said Pat.

"It's just an expression," said Crumples. "Like I scratch your back, you scratch mine."

"I still don't know what the hell you're talking about," said Pat.

"Look, son," said Crumples. "It's perfectly straight-forward. I need a story, a story nobody else has. You—well you're just a kid going to a city you don't know, you'll need money, someone to point you in the right direction, some-body to get you out of trouble if you get into it . . . you need a friend, I need a story. That's what I'm suggesting—a partnership. What do you think?"

Pat shrugged.

"Will you quit it with that damn shrugging?" Crumples snapped, then quickly produced the money Pat had origi-nally stolen from him from his wallet, and smoothed the crumples out of it. "Here," he said, holding it out to him, "a hundred and fifty euros. For that, you tell me every-thing, plus you get a friend for life. Or at least for a few days."

Pat looked at the money. Crumples was right—he was going to a strange city, he didn't know anyone and he cer-tainly didn't have any money. But, on the other hand, hav-ing his story splashed all over the papers was hardly going to help his quest to get the head back, and besides, there was something he didn't quite trust about this tired, stained-looking man now visibly beginning to sweat beside him. He was a reporter. He wanted a story. He wasn't a friend. He wasn't a friend like Sean. Sean might have beaten him up, but he was still the best friend he'd ever had.

Pat looked at the money again. He would have to eat. He would have to put his head down somewhere. There might be buses, other trains, people to bribe, information to buy. He *needed* the money.

Slowly he reached out and took it out of Crumples' hand.

Crumples smiled brightly. "Partners," he said.

Pat had decided that he had no alternative but to tell Crumples the absolute truth about his quest.

Or at least as much truth as he could make up.

"And your mother is really a polar explorer?"

"Absolutely. That's why I'm doing this by myself. See, she's away for half the year, up at the Pole. And what with my dad being killed by that elephant, there's nobody else to help me."

"And the elephant?"

"Well, they had to shoot it, didn't they? They kill any animal that kills a human. Even if it was an accident. The elephant just kind of sat down at the wrong time, right when my dad was kneeling to tie his shoe. You don't remember it? It was in all the papers—apart from one—the *Dublin Evening Herald*, they wouldn't do anything on it because the reason my dad was at the zoo in the first place is that he won a free behind-the-scenes tour of the zoo in a competition in the *Herald*. So they were really embarrassed about it because it was supposed to be such a special prize, and then the elephant went and sat on my dad and that kind of made the prize not quite as special as they'd hoped."

"And then what happened?"

"Well, they buried him. Although they needed a really big coffin. To get the trunk in."

"They buried the elephant in a coffin!"

Pat roared with laughter. "No, of course not! I was only joking. Do you think it's weird me making jokes about the elephant that killed my dad? I had to go and see a psychiatrist to see if I was dealing with it okay, and they thought it was a good sign that I could make jokes about it. About the elephant. I wouldn't make jokes about my dad. Because he's dead. And flat as a pancake too."

"This is *dynamite*!" Crumples exclaimed.

Pat smiled and sat back, half exhausted at the effort of making up such complete and utter nonsense. He had started out trying to be quite serious about it all, trying to construct a story that sounded like it might be true. But every time he opened his mouth something totally fantastical came out. Perhaps it was his lack of sleep. Or lack of food. Or the pure adrenaline of going off on an adventure on behalf of God. Perhaps all of these symptoms had combined to do funny things to his brain. But whatever it was he couldn't help himself. What was really freaking him out, though, was the fact that Crumples was writing it all down. He was taking it all seriously. If anyone was a moron, then Crumples was. Weren't reporters supposed to be able to sniff out rubbish when they heard it? Weren't they supposed to be cynical and world-weary? But Crumples was lapping it all up like a kitten at his first saucer of milk.

Crumples blew air out of his cheeks, and flipped his notebook to the next page. "Okay," he said, "now what about the head itself?"

"It's *spooky*," said Pat.

"What do you mean, spooky?"

"It glows in the dark, I swear to God."

Crumples duly noted this down. "And the men that stole it, you say their car had Belfast number plates?"

"Yeah. Absolutely."

"And can you remember the number?"

Pat opened his mouth a little, put a finger to his lip as if he was thinking. Crumples moved even closer; his tongue darted out to lick his bone-dry lips; Pat could see the little pulse in the side of his temple beating wildly; he was *so* excited. He was about to get some vital information no other reporter in either country had, information that could possibly help crack the case.

"The license plate number?" Pat asked.

"*Yes*," Crumples wheezed.

"From the back of the getaway car?"

"*Yes* . . ." He inched closer again.

"Sorry," said Pat, "can't just remember it." Crumples looked suddenly deflated. "But . . . ," Pat added quickly, "it might come back to me."

This little germ of hope was enough to light Crumples up again. He looked back down at his notes. "This is great stuff," he said, "great stuff."

By now the train was beginning to pull into Belfast Central Station. All around businessmen were standing up, stretching, yawning, then clawing their briefcases back down from the luggage racks above them. Pat stood up too. He had a hundred and fifty euros in his pocket. Now all he had to do was lose the reporter and he could get on with his quest.

As if he could tell what Pat was thinking, Crumples put a protective hand on his shoulder and said, "All I need for you to do now is to come with me to the office, and we can take your photograph. Can't have an article without a little piccy, can we?"

Pat smiled and nodded.

But he wasn't going to any newspaper office. He knew that much. He didn't need his mug plastered all over the paper. And besides, whoever ran the paper would take one look at the story and realize he'd taken Crumples for a ride; what was more, he'd say we can't support this kid in this crazy mission, he should be at home with his parents. They'd lock him in a room until the police came.

Pat climbed down from the train with Crumples, and allowed himself to be guided up the sloping walkway to the ticket collection point. When they'd passed through it Pat quickly scanned around the main concourse. He spotted the toilets on his right.

"I need to pee," he said quickly.

Crumples nodded and crossed to the toilets. He was about to enter them with him, until Pat said, "Alone." Crumples, aware that grown men going into toilets with little boys who weren't their children was often grounds for arrest, stopped by the entrance and produced his mobile phone. "I'll phone the office," he said, "get them to send a car."

Pat nodded and entered the toilets.

There were four cubicles, a long white urinal, and several wash hand basins. But there was no obvious way for him to sneak out. There were windows, but they were shut and barred. He cursed to himself.

There was nothing else for it.

It was time to use something that all boys are aware of, and many girls.

Pat was aware of it. Eddie was aware of it.

"Oh, Mr. Matchitt," Pat called. "Can I show you something?"

Crumples called back somewhat hesitantly from the entrance. "Show me . . . ?"

"In here, I think it might be a clue. . . ."

"A clue?"

There was a sudden note of excitement in his voice. He came hurrying into the toilets and found Pat standing in the middle of the floor, pointing up at the ceiling.

"Look," said Pat, "is that what I think it is?"

Crumples stood beside him and squinted up. His eyes searched back and forth.

"What . . . do . . . you . . . think . . . it . . . is . . . ?" he asked in a puzzled tone.

"A ceiling," Pat said, and whacked Crumples in the willy. There was a moment when absolutely nothing happened. But it was a very short moment.

Crumples screamed, and crumpled to the ground.

Pat took off like a rocket to begin his search for the head of Oliver Plunkett.

Seven

Eddie tramped toward Brown's Academy. All around him there were boys in similarly loud purple uniforms, boys with equally miserable faces. But theirs was a different kind of misery, the kind of misery brought on merely by having to return to school a week before every other kid in the city. Eddie's misery was on an altogether grander scale. Captain Black's power and influence seemed to know no bounds. He'd made sure Eddie had been denied access to his schools of choice, and then arranged for him to become a pupil at Brown's Academy—while all the time making it appear that Eddie's mum had somehow organized it herself. Captain Black had changed Eddie's entire education, in fact his entire life, because he wanted some information about another boy attending the school. Why couldn't he just have chosen Bacon or Bap or any other of the hundreds of Reservoir Pups?

Why pick on me?

Because he hates me.

Because he's jealous of what I did to the baby-snatchers.

Because he wants to make my life a misery.

As Eddie passed through the school gates—they were big, metal, rusting gates, standing open, behind which a driveway curved away around to the left before disappearing through a bank of trees—he took out the envelope Bacon and Bap had given him and ripped it open. Inside there was a small card with the name **IVAN CUTLER** written in red ink. Red. Very dramatic. Who did Captain Black think he was? Did he think he could just issue commands and expect Eddie to obey them? So what if they gave him a hard time when he was going home from school! Hadn't he faced up to the baby-snatchers and defeated them? He would find a way to beat Captain Black and the Reservoir Pups as well. Eddie tore the card in two and threw it to the ground.

There.

Stuff you, Captain Black.

"HEY! YOU! BOY!"

Eddie looked up to find a man in a gray suit, with a black cape billowing in the wind behind him, bearing down on him. He had an eagle's beak of a face. His skin was blotched red with anger. All around Eddie, boys backed away.

"What's your name?" the man demanded.

"Eddie," said Eddie.

"Eddie what!" the man exploded.

"Eddie Malone."

"What class are you in?"

"Don't know."

The man rolled his eyes. He delved into his jacket pocket and took out a small notebook and pen. "Eddie Malone," he repeated as he wrote the name down. He snapped it quickly shut. "Eddie Malone—you're in detention. Today. Littering. Three-fifteen until five. My room."

The man spun on his heel and hurried away.

Eddie stood there, stunned. He'd been a pupil at Brown's Academy for just over fifteen seconds—since he'd walked through the gates—and he was already in detention. Eddie shook himself, then bent down and picked up the torn card. He was about to slip the card and its torn envelope into his blazer pocket when someone spoke from behind.

"No—let me."

Eddie turned to find a boy with thick curly hair and thick, thick glasses smiling crookedly at him. He nodded down at the torn card and envelope and put out his hand. Eddie hesitantly handed over the paper—and the boy immediately produced a lighter from his pocket and set fire to them.

Eddie glanced quickly around, terrified in case the same teacher spotted the flames—but there was no sign of him. The boy let the card and envelope fall to the ground an instant before the flames reached his fingers, and then they both watched as they curled into each other and burned away into black cinders before drifting away on the breeze. The boy grinned at Eddie again and said, "First day, eh?"

Eddie nodded ruefully. "Who *was* that?" he asked, nodding back in the direction the teacher had gone.

"No idea," said the boy, "my first day as well."

"Oh," said Eddie.

The boy nodded, and they stood there somewhat awkwardly for several moments. Then the other boy put out his hand and said, "I'm Gilmore."

"Is that your first name?"

"Sorry," the boy said. "My brother used to go here, he said they never use your first name. So I guess I'm just plain Gilmore."

Eddie clasped his hand and said, "Well then, I'm Eddie."

Gilmore smiled again, nodded, and said, "Then I'm Gary."

They walked on up the driveway together. Eddie had imagined that Brown's Academy, with its fancy name and its roster of rich pupils, would be an ancient and impressive building, more castle than school, but when they emerged from the shadow of the trees he was disappointed to see an undistinguished gray building surrounded by a dozen or more Portakabins. To the left there were several rugby pitches. To the right a hockey pitch. Between them there was a playground covered in gravel. It was really very unimpressive.

Eddie stood with Gary waiting for the bell to sound. They didn't really know what to say to each other. Eventually Eddie said: "So what does your dad do?"

"Don't have one," said Gary.

"Oh."

"IIe's dead."

"Oh. Right."

"What about yours?"

"He doesn't do anything. He's . . ." He was going to say he's run away to England with Spaghetti Legs, forcing me to leave my home, my school, my friends, forcing me to move to a dark and dangerous city, forcing me into the arms of the Reservoir Pups, forcing me to take on a dangerous gang of baby-snatchers . . . but that seemed a bit much to burden a complete stranger with. So he said: ". . . he's dead as well."

"Oh," said Gary. "Sorry."

"Sorry too," said Eddie.

Then the bell rang and half a dozen teachers, wearing identical gray suits and flowing black capes, emerged to usher them through the double doors and down a dark corridor into a large hall where the boys quickly formed up into their respective years, and then classes. Eddie and Gary stood together, a little bit lost, until the teacher who'd given Eddie detention came over and pointed them in the direction of a large group of boys on the far side of the hall. They walked somewhat nervously across.

"Is this the Second Form?" Eddie asked the first boy they came to, a tall, gangly kid with lots of spots on his face.

"No, it's a training camp for Manchester United," the boy snapped back, and then cackled at his great wit, and turned away to talk to his friends. Eddie turned to Gary and shrugged. But another boy who'd overheard came up beside them and said, "Sure, this is Second Form. Whose class are you in?"

"Don't know yet," said Eddie.

The boy, who had short red hair and a long nose, nodded toward the back of the group where a teacher was ticking names off on a clipboard. The teacher could only have been about four and a half feet tall. In fact he was smaller than most of the boys around him. He had short blond hair and glasses and a soft, childish face; he wore a blond mustache on his lip, possibly in an attempt to make himself look older, but in fact he just looked like a boy who'd stuck a small blond mustache on his lip in an attempt to make himself look older. The red-haired boy bent to Eddie's ear and whispered, "His name's Mr. Short. Ironic, yeah?"

Eddie nodded.

"You better go and get signed up."

Eddie walked with Gary across to Mr. Short, who finished ticking off the other boys, then glanced up at them. "Well?" he said.

"Don't know what class we're in, Mr. Short," said Eddie.

Mr. Short's eyes narrowed. His cheeks flushed. "What did you say?"

Eddie, who should perhaps have known better, said, "Don't know what class we're in, Mr. Short."

Mr. Short bit down on his lip. "Your names?" They gave them quickly. He raised his clipboard and made the relevant ticks, then glared at them again. "I'll tell you which class you're in," he snarled. "You're in the detention class! Today! Three-fifteen to five o'clock in my room! And my name is not Mr. Short!"

And with that he flounced away, accompanied by the laughs and giggles of the rest of the form. Eddie stood there, fuming. Gary took several steps away from him and gave him a look that said, "You seem to be dangerous to know."

Then a bell rang and very quickly the hall emptied, leaving Eddie and Gary standing alone in the middle of it, not quite sure where they were supposed to be, or who they were supposed to ask, and feeling absolutely that the last place on earth they really wanted to be was right there in Brown's Academy.

Eventually they were assigned their classes. Eddie worked out by a process of elimination that the teacher who'd given him his first detention was called Smithins, and that his form teacher, Mr. Short, was actually called Welch. Eddie's first class was Religious Education with a Miss Danvers, and Gary's first was with Mr Whittles. Eddie was thinking how pretty and friendly Miss Danvers was, because she'd had to come and collect him from the hall and had chatted away to him like an old friend all the way to the door of the class. But as soon as she was inside she changed abruptly, became much more serious and disciplined. She made him stand up at the front to introduce himself to his classmates. He decided not to mention the baby-snatchers and the fact that he was a gang leader intent on world domination; or indeed that he was addicted to Jaffa cakes. He just said his name was

Eddie and he was new to Belfast and he was interested in football and movies and PlayStation 2.

"Well, that's just marvelous, Eddie," Miss Danvers said with a warm smile, then waved around the class, "I'm sure you'll be made to feel quite at home." Gary Gilmore had clearly been misinformed. Here was one teacher at least who cared enough about her pupils to call them by their first name.

"Craig?" Miss Danvers nodded at the boy who'd made fools of them with the erroneous Mr. Short. "Craig, perhaps you could make sure Eddie gets to know the school, and gets his class timetable sorted out?"

Craig nodded unhappily.

"And, Eddie," Miss Danvers asked, "you do believe in God and the Ten Commandments?"

Eddie, rather surprised by this, cleared his throat and uttered a rather vague, "Uhm, yes."

"Excellent!" Miss Danvers clapped her hands together. "Then you can join my Bible class. It's this afternoon from three-fifteen until five."

"I'd love to . . ."

"Excellent!"

"Unfortunately, I'm in detention."

Miss Danvers' brow furrowed. "How can you be in detention? This is the first class of the first day of the new term."

Eddie shrugged.

"Who are you in detention with?" asked Miss Danvers.

Eddie cleared his throat again. "Mr. Smithins," he said, and just as Miss Danvers was about to respond, he added, "and Mr. Welch."

Miss Danvers smiled indulgently. "Eddie, it's either one or the other."

"No, it's both."

Miss Danvers put her hands on her hips. "I see," she said. She moved closer. She wasn't smiling now. Her lips were very red and her teeth were very white. She spoke quietly, but her words were suddenly heavy with menace and threat. "Well, I'll have you know that I don't tolerate troublemakers in my class."

"I'm not a—"

"Be quiet!" Eddie fell silent. She spoke quickly and sharply. "I believe in the Christian values of peace, love and understanding, Eddie, but that doesn't mean I'm a soft touch. I do not tolerate indiscipline, violent behavior, bullying, laziness or failure to apply oneself to one's studies. However, you will be pleased to know that I do not believe in detention. Obviously your detention schedule is already busy enough." Eddie was about to give a thankful smile when she added: "What I do believe in is Bloody Hell."

Eddie blinked at her.

"Do you know what Bloody Hell is?"

"I . . ."

"I'll tell you what Bloody Hell is." She turned to her desk and pulled open a drawer. She delved inside and produced a short but solid block of wood. She crossed back to him and held the block up. It was crisscrossed with fine lines and scarred with bumps and knots. "Do you know why this is called the Bloody Hell?"

Eddie shook his head. The class had grown noticeably quiet behind him.

"Well, Eddie, I believe in biblical punishments. An eye for an eye, a tooth for a tooth. You do something wrong and you will pay for it. Put out your hand."

Eddie put out his hand. He looked at the block of wood. She . . . wouldn't . . . she couldn't . . .

But she did.

She raised the block, then whacked him with it.

Eddie reeled away clutching his hand. It was completely numb. It felt like there were several broken bones in it. He squeezed it into his armpit for safekeeping.

"And that's why we call it the Bloody Hell," said his teacher, her voice as cool as ice. "You've had one stroke just to say hello. Cause trouble in my class, Eddie Malone, and the minimum punishment is five strokes." She set the Bloody Hell back on her desk, then clapped her hands together quite happily. "Now, children, we're going to talk about the importance of love in the Christian family."

Eddie tramped down the aisle to his desk.

He sat massaging his hand, reflecting, between whimpers, on the fact that it had not been the most wonderful start to his first day at Brown's Academy. In fact, it had been so bad, he could only content himself with the knowledge that things could not possibly get any worse.

Eight

It was a strange new city for Pat, bigger than Drogheda, smaller than Dublin, but he was an orphan and well used to fending for himself. That was one thing you had to be able to do in the orphanage. Sure, he had friends like Sean, but when it came down to survival, he only had himself to rely on, and he reckoned he was pretty good at it. Wasn't he in Belfast under his own steam? Hadn't he hoodwinked a journalist out of a hundred and fifty euros? Wasn't he standing in the middle of Royal Avenue munching on a sausage roll and drinking a Coke? Wasn't he on a mission from God?

Pat was halfway through his sausage roll when he saw the primate.

Not that he was to be seen striding through the early-morning shoppers—but there he was, all the same, about twelve inches tall, talking on the television screen in the Dixons front window. Pat pushed through the door into the shop and hurried across to the TV section where he found the primate on about a dozen different screens, talking to reporters. The sound was turned low, but Pat could just make it out.

"Oliver Plunkett lost his head because of his beliefs," the primate was saying, "because he would not bow before the tyranny of the English monarchy. I do not believe that we should bow before this form of tyranny either." He held up a piece of paper and shook his head. "We will not pay this three million euros."

Three million euros. Pat's mouth dropped open; crumbs of sausage roll made a bid for freedom. Three million . . . he jumped suddenly as a hand was brought down on his shoulder. "Excuse me, son," a woman in a gray uniform said, "are you with someone?"

Pat pointed vaguely across the shop. "My mum," he said, managing to shower the woman with flakes of puff pastry.

"Okay—but no eating in the shop, all right?"

Pat nodded and pushed what was left of the sausage roll into his mouth. "All gone," he said, although actually it sounded like "Allthgonth." The security guard didn't look very impressed. She lifted a TV remote control off one of the sets and switched the channel. Immediately the dozen screens lost the primate, and found the *Teletubbies*. She gave Pat a sarcastic smile and walked away.

Three million euros.

My God.

That was two million, nine hundred and ninety nine thousand, eight hundred and fifty-two euros more than he had in his pocket. (He had spent one euro on the sausage roll and one on the Coke.)

Somebody expected the primate to pay that much to get the head of Oliver Plunkett back. A moldy old head that looked like a coconut.

"Sorry, God," Pat said quickly for thinking of Oliver Plunkett once again as a moldy old coconut. "Sorry, God," he said again for thinking that he had thought of Oliver Plunkett once again as a moldy old coconut. Doh! He'd thought it again. . . .

Pat snapped himself out of it. He went outside. Three million euros! The primate had said he wasn't going to pay it—but even to make such a demand, it showed how valuable some people considered Oliver Plunkett's head to be. Or at least how important it was to the primate. Pat thought back to what the primate had told him in the church. That the pope was coming, that he feared the theft of the head was an attempt to embarrass him, to prevent him from becoming the next pope. Pat knew now, more than ever before, how vital the head was to the primate. Even so—the fact that he had gone public with the ransom note meant that he wasn't prepared to just buy it back, he wasn't prepared to concede to the demands of the thieves.

To Pat that meant only one thing—*he's relying on me. I am the one man—boy—that stands between him and complete and utter humiliation.*

I will get the head.

I will return it.

So Pat, armed with only one clue, set his master plan for recovering the stolen head of Oliver Plunkett into motion.

He started to cry.

It was only a sniffle at first.

Then it was more of a series of connected sobs.

Then it became a great wailing. . . .

At first the passing shoppers just looked at him.

Then one woman stopped and asked if he was okay.

Which was a stupid question, but he didn't say that, he just kept on roaring. A small group of women tried to console him, but he kept at it until eventually, eventually, a policeman came sauntering across and bent down before him.

"What's the matter, son?" he asked.

"I'm lost!" Pat wailed.

"Oh dear . . . where's your mum?"

"She's at home! I sneaked out because I wanted to go to the toy shop! But I'm lost and I don't know how to get home!"

The policeman smiled warmly. "Well—now, that's nothing to worry about, is it? Sure can't we get you home!"

Pat cut the wailing, and sniffed up. "Could you?" he said.

"Course we can!"

Pat even managed the beginnings of a smile.

"Now then, just give me your address and we'll have you home in no time!" Pat allowed his face to collapse into tears again. "What is it, son?" the policeman asked.

"We've just moved house! I've forgotten my new address!"

The policeman blew air out of his cheeks. "I see. That makes it slightly more difficult then. . . ." He could see that Pat was building toward another of his wails, so he quickly grasped him by the shoulders and said, "But don't worry, son, I'm not a policeman for nothing. We can solve this together. What we need are some clues—are you with me, son?"

Pat nodded.

"Now then . . . what's your name?"

"Pat."

"Yes—Pat, but Pat what, what's your surname?"

"I can't remember."

"You can't remember your name?"

"My mum just got married again, that's why we've moved house, and I can't remember my new surname! My new dad's first name is . . . Olivor . . . but I'm sorry I just can't . . ." He started the tears again.

"Oh, shush now, shush," said the policeman, "we're not done yet, are we? All we need is a different clue. Now then, is there anything you can tell me, anything that might help?"

Pat started to shake his head—then brightened suddenly, as if the thought had just come to him—"I remember our number plate!"

"Your car number plate?" Pat nodded enthusiastically. "Well, that's a start!"

Pat quickly gave him the number of the vehicle the men who had stolen the head of Oliver Plunkett had used to make their getaway. The policeman lifted his radio and called the number in. A couple of minutes later a response came back via the earphone he was wearing. He looked at Pat. "Twenty-one Warleggen Crescent?"

"That's it!" said Pat.

"Okay then, mystery solved. Now what about getting you home? You wouldn't mind a ride in a police car, would you?"

Pat smiled like a little kid.

Nine

Eddie had double detention and had made enemies of three teachers and it was still only lunchtime. There was plenty of time left to get into even more trouble. He stood stiffly in the playground while hundreds of kids charged around him enjoying their break from lessons. The only other boy he knew was Gary Gilmore, and although Eddie had already made two complete circuits of the school grounds looking for him, he was nowhere to be found. *He's probably hiding.* Eddie stared down the drive toward the trees; hidden behind them were the school gates. He could just start walking now. Surely if he arrived home with his tales of woe his mum would understand that Brown's Academy wasn't for him.

That was, if he even got home.

The Reservoir Pups would surely be waiting for him somewhere between the school gates and his apartment.

There is a saying: sticks and stones will break your bones, but names will never hurt you.

Eddie wasn't worried about the names. He was worried about the sticks and stones. And knives and guns and whatever else the Reservoir Pups had in store for him. He sighed. All this because Captain Black wanted information about some idiot called Ivan Cutler.

Eddie looked around the playground and wondered which boy it was. Was he the tall blond guy running with the football at his feet? Or was he the little fat lad eating crisps and chewing gum at the same time? Was he the punk with the spiky hair reading a *Marvel* comic? What about the long-haired kid secretly smoking behind one of the Portakabins?

Eddie jumped suddenly as he was poked in the back. It was his classmate Craig, and he didn't look like he was about to ask Eddie if they could be best friends. "Dopey Danvers told me to make sure you know your way around the school," he said.

Eddie nodded.

Craig began to point: "There's the playground, there's the science block, there's the Portakabins, there's the rugby pitch and there's the gates. Okay?"

As a tour guide he seemed to lack something. He started to turn away. "You wouldn't happen to know—?" Eddie began.

"*What?*" Craig snapped back, his mouth curling up in irritation.

"I'm looking for Ivan Cutler."

Craig's irritated mouth smoothed out into a sarcastic smile. "And he's looking for you."

Then he stalked off before Eddie could ask him what he meant.

Eddie blew air out of his cheeks and walked off in the other direction. Why was everyone at Brown's Academy in such foul form? He knew money couldn't buy happiness, but they could certainly afford to buy a few lessons in politeness.

Eddie began his third tour of the school grounds. He skirted the football field, then walked along the back of the Portakabins. The boy he'd seen smoking a few minutes before was just in the act of lighting another one when he spotted Eddie watching him.

"What?" he snapped.

"Nothing."

"Good. Then get lost."

"I'm looking for Ivan Cutler."

The boy glared at him for a moment and then said: "And I hear he's looking for you too."

Eddie walked on, even more confused. Once, and it could have been a mistake, but twice? *Ivan Cutler's looking for me. My God, what has Captain Black done? What has he told Ivan Cutler about me? Is this how he's getting his revenge? Not content with sending me to some school for rich kids where I stick out like a sore thumb, he's also told the school mad boy some outrageous lie about me and now he's looking for me. He's going to beat me to a pulp. Swell.*

My life is just so wonderful.

Eddie massaged his hand. There was still a dull throb coming from it. He had been struck with a block of wood by his teacher! Surely there was some law against that? What sort of a school had he come to? Where nobody had a nice word, where detentions were handed out for the slightest offense, where teachers beat you with huge trees? His stomach rumbled suddenly. Naturally, just to complete his wonderful day, Eddie had forgotten to bring a packed lunch, and he only had enough money for his train fare home. He was starving. He had a sore hand. He had no friends.

He wanted to go home.

Eddie, it's only your first day, his mum would say, and send him right back.

He glanced at his watch. Another ten minutes until class started. But there was no harm in being early. He wandered into the science block and counted down five rooms to where Dr. Griffin was due to take his class for chemistry. The door was already open. In his other schools the doors had been kept locked between classes, but perhaps rich kids were different. Perhaps they didn't destroy things when left to their own devices. Eddie stood in the doorway and peered in; if the teacher was already there he'd seek permission to enter; if there were other kids, then he'd join them. He'd not had a chance to speak to many of them so far; perhaps this brief period before class started would be his chance to make his first friends.

But there was no teacher, and there was only one boy, and he wasn't even in Eddie's class. He was standing behind a table at the back which was covered in flasks and tubes and vials, and they were all bubbling away. Eddie glanced up at the door to make sure he was indeed at the right classroom. He was.

"Gary?" said Eddie. Gary Gilmore looked up. With his crooked smile and curly hair and big, big glasses, Gary looked just the way a mad professor would look in a cartoon. Except madder. "Hiya, Freddie," he said.

"Eddie," said Eddie. "What, ahm, exactly are you doing?"

"Oh, just messin'," said Gary.

It looked like a very complicated form of messing

Eddie moved into the class. Immediately he noticed a strong sulfurous smell, and as he drew closer he became aware of an intense heat coming from the bubbling flasks.

"Have you been kept in or something?" he asked. "Is this some sort of detention?"

"Oh no," said Gary, lifting a test tube and pouring a pink solution into an already smoking flask of green liquid, "I do this for fun. Not really the sporty type—but this I can do all day."

Eddie nodded down at the table. "And what . . . exactly . . . *is* this?"

"I'm building a thermonuclear device."

"You're *what*?"

Gary giggled—a bizarre sort of noise which sounded like air escaping from a leaking tire. "Only joking," he said. "I'm just trying to create a new soft drink—you know, like Coke or Sprite or something."

Eddie nodded. He supposed there was no harm in it. The nearest he'd come to ever conducting an experiment was combining jam, peanut butter and several Jaffa cakes in a sandwich, and then toasting it. It was remarkably successful. But it wasn't exactly science. And from what he knew about Coke or Sprite or any other drink or food that ended up in Tesco's market, they were usually created by huge teams of highly paid scientists. Not by schoolboys in loud purple blazers.

"That's, uh . . . very interesting, Gary . . . I take it . . . the, uh, teachers do know that you're in here?"

"Well," said Gary, "not exactly . . . but I mean . . . they're all for us being enthusiastic about our work, aren't they? Besides, what harm can it do?"

Eddie shuddered. The words "what harm can it do" always got that reaction from him, because he recognized them as FAMOUS LAST WORDS. He looked nervously back at the door. Then at his watch.

"Don't you . . . have a class to go to?" he asked.

It was a bad thing to ask, because Gary had a flask of black liquid in his watch hand. Without thinking he twisted his wrist to look at the time, and managed to spill the contents of the flask out over the desk and the vials and the tubes and the glass flasks before him.

"Oh . . ." Gary's brow furrowed and his pink skin began to lose its color. "Oh dear," he said.

"Oh dear?" Eddie asked nervously.

"That wasn't the brightest thing to do."

"Why . . . have you ruined your experiment?"

"Well, yes, kind of." Gary's eyes widened and fixed on the chemicals before him. They had been merely bubbling before, but now they were definitely bubbling *up*. There had been steam coming from them before, but now it seemed to be thickening and darkening. No longer steam—but *smoke*. "I think . . . I think . . . I think there's going to be an"—and suddenly he dashed out from behind the desk—"explosion!"

He grabbed Eddie's arm as he passed and dragged him toward the door. Behind them a weird shriek came from one of the flasks, like a boiling kettle which someone had forgotten to switch off; and then just as they ducked through the doorway and pressed themselves against the wall in the hall outside, there was a huge explosion. The wall they were leaning against actually vibrated.

"Oh lordy," said Gary.

Above them a smoke alarm began to wail; they chanced a look back into the room and saw that not only had the explosion destroyed every piece of equipment in the lab and smashed all of the windows, but it had also managed to set fire to the curtains.

"What do we do?" Eddie shouted.

Thick black smoke was already beginning to seep out into the corridor.

"We run!" Gary shouted, and proceeded to do just that.

Eddie stood frozen in shock for a moment. Double detention, the enmity of three teachers, and now he'd inadvertently helped to set the school on fire! And he was still standing there like he was waiting for a bus!

Eddie shook himself and ran after Gary.

He was three-quarters of the way up the corridor, with

the smoke chasing after him and the smoke alarm sounding urgently above him, when a boy's voice called, "What is it? What's going on?" from a classroom on his right.

Eddie shouted, "There's a fire! Get out!" but kept running.

"Help me!"

"Help yourself!" Eddie shouted back.

"HELP ME!" the boy demanded again.

Eddie paused by the double doors leading out to the playground. There was no sign of the boy emerging from his class.

"Just run, you bloody eejit!" Eddie yelled back. "The school's on fire! What are you, blind or stupid?"

"Blind!" the boy shouted back.

"What?"

"I'm blind. Which way?"

Eddie glanced through the glass doors. Teachers were hurrying toward him, pupils were standing in groups, watching dumbly as their school began to burn.

Blind?

Eddie didn't even think about it. He took a deep breath, then dashed back along the corridor through the now choking black smoke toward the boy's classroom. He ducked inside it—and was relieved to find that the smoke had not yet fully penetrated this room. Toward the back of the class, beside the windows, he saw a boy wearing sunglasses standing rooted to the spot. Eddie'd spotted him that morning in the assembly hall and presumed he was just a cool guy who loved his shades. "This way!" Eddie shouted. But the boy stayed where he was, too frightened to move. So Eddie crossed the room and took the boy's arm and led him through the jumble of desks back out toward the corridor.

But the smoke there had become even thicker.

"What's wrong, what's happening, what's going on?" The boy's anxious words all came out in a panicky burst. He grabbed at Eddie. "I can't breathe!"

"Don't worry," Eddie said.

"Smoke . . . burning . . . we're going to die!"

Eddie coughed, and peered into the growing darkness. He could feel the smoke burning inside his chest and knew instinctively that it was now too thick for them. Eddie pushed the boy back into the classroom.

"What're you doing?" the blind boy demanded. "We're going to burn in here!"

"Not if I can help it!"

Eddie lifted a chair from behind the nearest desk, then hurled it through the classroom window. It was a big window, and it made a big noise as it shattered. But they were rewarded with a blast of cool air which ushered what smoke was seeping into the room back out into the corridor.

"What was that? What was that? What's going on?" the boy cried.

"It's our way out," said Eddie.

He guided him to the smashed window, then helped him climb up and out onto the windowsill, where Eddie quickly joined him. Then they both jumped down into the playground, where they knelt coughing on the graveled tarmac. Pupils gathered around and looked at them curiously. The smoke alarm continued to sound; some-where in the background a fire engine's siren could be heard.

Then the eagle-faced Mr. Smithins burst through the growing crowd of onlookers. "I saw what happened!" he exclaimed. Miss Danvers also appeared through the crush and immediately bent to help the blind boy back to his feet.

Eddie, his throat dry and raspy, his chest sore from coughing, tried desperately to think of an excuse, but he couldn't focus.

Smithins suddenly grabbed his arm and pulled Eddie up from the tarmac. Then he took hold of his shoulders.

"I'm sorr—" Eddie began weakly, but Smithins imme-diately cut him off:

"You saved Ivan Cutler's life!" he cried. "You're a bloody hero!"

Ten

The police car came to a halt at the far end of Warloggen Crescent, a long terrace of tall red-bricked buildings in the west of the city. Pat had by now finished eating the doughnut and drinking the Coke the cops had bought him. He wiped the sprinkle of sugar from the sides of his mouth and said plainly that no, he didn't need them to walk him up to his front door, he was probably in enough trouble already without him being seen to be brought home by the police. So they said their goodbyes and told him to look after himself and drove happily away, pleased that they could help such a nice kid out, pleased that they could do something good and decent in a city that usually called on them only when there was something horrible to deal with or someone violent to be subdued.

Pat watched them go from the corner of the crescent.

He felt a bit bad that he'd told them a little white lie—well, actually no, he'd lied through his teeth. But it was all in a good cause.

Twenty-one Warleggen Crescent.

He walked up past it as nonchalantly as possible. There was a small square of overgrown front garden. The window frames had once been blue, but were now badly chipped or peeling. The windows themselves were dirty, but he could still make out the age-thin curtains and yellowed blinds. It didn't look to him much like a family home. There was no suggestion that there was a woman or wife or mother living there, or if there was she had no interest in cleaning or painting or doing the garden. Pat had no mother, and so tended to have an idealized vision of what a mother should be, and indeed what a father should be. A man was a man, and a wife made stew. A man went out to work and a woman kept house. The man was big and strong and the woman looked after the kids. Pat probably knew that the real world wasn't always or even usually like that, but that was what he preferred to imagine. Twenty-one Warleggen Crescent looked neglected, and he supposed it was being neglected by a single man without a woman to look after him. Or indeed, a car to drive about in.

Pat's thinking was this: the people who'd stolen the head of Oliver Plunkett obviously weren't stupid enough to use their own car, but the chances were that they'd stolen one from the area where they lived. Why travel miles to steal a car when there's probably one on your own doorstep? Secondly—usually to steal a car you have to break a window or bust a lock. But if you were going to commit a major crime you couldn't take the chance of some passing police officer noticing that you were driving a car with a broken window or spotting a hole where the door lock had been punched out. No— you needed your car to look completely normal, like you were just out for a nice drive. So that meant that you had to have the keys—which you could either steal from the car owner or force him to hand over. Now, even down in his orphanage in Drogheda Pat was aware of how dark and dangerous Belfast was, that there were always bombings, and shootings and murders. So it seemed to him that if a gang of robbers knocked on your door one night and demanded that you give them your car, the chances were that you would hand over the keys without much of a protest. And the chances were also that you would get a good look at whoever was stealing your car. Because they'd know you'd be too frightened to tell the police.

So that was Pat's plan.

To try to find out from the owner of the stolen car who the robbers were, and if they lived locally.

Dead simple.

Really.

What could be easier?

Just knock on the door and say, excuse me, did some men happen to steal your car the other night, and did you get a good look at them?

And he'd say—sure they did, and here are their addresses.

Pat sighed. Okay. So it maybe wouldn't be quite that simple.

But he had to try.

God, the pope, the primate and all of Ireland's Catholics were depending on him. Pat walked up to the door and knocked. When there was no response after thirty seconds he raised his fist to knock again, but before it could make contact with the wood the door opened suddenly before him—although by just a fraction. Two eyes peered warily out of the darkness of the hall. "What?" a rough voice asked. "Whaddya want?"

"I was—"

"Whatever you're selling I don't want, whatever you want, I'm not interested, just go away."

The man—and he presumed it was a man, not just a woman with a big deep growl of a voice—slammed the door.

But Pat wasn't going to give up that easily. He knocked again. When the door reopened he immediately launched into: "I'm not selling anything, I just wanted to know if you'd seen—"

He didn't get any further. The door was opened fully and a big man in a big vest, with tattoos on his arms and thick stubble on his face, poked him hard in the chest. "What've you got, cloth ears or something? I told you to go away. So bugger off!" The man poked him again, forcing Pat to take several steps backward, then slammed the door hard.

Pat stood there, quite shocked, for several moments. But then his head began to clear. It seemed the man didn't want to talk. Which meant, clearly, that either he was too *scared* to talk—or he had something to hide.

Of course he could just have been a nasty and horrible man.

But somehow, Pat didn't think so.

He walked to the end of the crescent; there was a shop on the corner with a wall outside it he could sit on. He bought a bag of sweets and sat there for about an hour watching the house while trying to work out what his next move should be. If the man did have something to hide, then he had to find out what it was. And that would mean finding out *who* he was, what he did, who his friends were, listening to his conversations, waiting all the time for him to give away some vital snippet of information that would direct Pat toward the secret hiding place of the head of Oliver Plunkett.

But what if he never came out?

What if the man was actually part of the gang?

Or what if the gang who'd stolen his car had also forced him to guard the head with his life? Maybe that was why he was so jumpy!

Pat had a decision to make—wait for the man to come out and then follow him, or search his house for clues.

Neither would be easy. Both would be dangerous.

In the end, though, he didn't have to make the decision at all, because as he sat watching the house and weighing up his options a taxi drew up outside, honked its horn, and a moment later the big man, now wearing scruffy jeans and a loose pullover, hurried out, slammed the door and jumped into the vehicle. Before Pat could even think about running after it, it had turned onto the main road and disappeared from view.

So there was no longer a choice—the house it was to be.

But not through the front door—it was too big and solid, and besides he could hardly walk up to it in broad daylight and crack it open with one of his expert kung fu kicks. Not that he had any expert kung fu kicks. Or even any ordinary ones. Pat couldn't fight his way out of a paper bag.

Instead he peered behind the corner shop, and saw that there was a glass-strewn alley leading down to the left along the rear of Warleggen Crescent. He hurried down this, using the wheelie bins with the house numbers painted on them to guide him to number twenty-one. There he found a wooden fence with several gaping holes in it. Pat stared through the holes at the house for several minutes, watching every single one of the back windows for any signs of movement from within. Then he darted through one of the holes into a small yard. He approached the back door and cautiously tried the handle—but it was locked.

Pat stepped back and looked up. There were three— no, four floors. There was a window slightly open on the second floor—if he could get up there, then maybe he could gain entry to the house. A drainpipe ran up the full length of the house close to the open window—but it looked old and brittle. Still—he was light enough, maybe it would hold his weight.

Only one way to find out.

Pat climbed onto the lowest windowsill and peered in at a small cluttered kitchen with a big pile of empty pizza boxes sitting by the sink. From the windowsill he cautiously put one foot on the circular rim which fitted one section of the drainpipe to the next and tried his weight. Good. It seemed strong enough. Then he chanced his full weight on it. Again it held—just. There was a bit of a shake.

One step at a time, one foot after the other, Pat hauled himself up.

The pipe was definitely shaking now—and he could see why. It had once been held tightly in place by three brackets—but two of them had clearly rusted away, and the third looked like it could go at any moment.

But he was halfway there.

He had to keep going.

The higher he went, the worse the shaking got.

Rattle.

Shake.

Screech.

Shudder.

As Pat climbed, flakes of rust began to rain down on him. Each step up he took was forcing the loose pipe hard against the brittle bracket; the closer he got to the window, the closer he got to the bracket and the greater the vibration against it.

Still he kept going.

Then he was level with the second floor window ledge—but not so close that he could just move sideways onto it. He would have to use the pipe to launch himself; and now that he was right up beside the bracket he could see that it had all but disintegrated. There was nothing now keeping the pipe upright but a few flakes of rust and fresh air. Pat looked at the ground below—had he really climbed that high? He was soaked through with sweat. He examined the windowsill again. It wasn't that great a jump—but it was awkward.

The pipe gave another shudder.

Even if he decided against breaking into the house, there was no way that the pipe would support him while he climbed back down again. It was either jump now or the pipe would collapse under him and he would fall with it. His head, and the rest of him, would shatter on the hard concrete below.

He had to go *now*—he had no choice.

Pat took a deep breath, then propelled himself sideways, using the pipe for leverage.

Even as he reached out for the windowsill the pipe gave way, split into three sections and fell away beneath him. As it clattered toward the ground Pat grasped the window ledge and held on for dear life. Below him the pipe struck the ground and exploded violently into a thousand pieces.

He might as well have shouted HELLO, I'M A BUR-GLAR at the top of his voice.

Using every last vestige of strength, Pat hauled himself up onto the ledge, pulled open the window, then tumbled through a set of closed curtains into the room below. Outside he could hear doors opening and dogs barking. He sat in the darkness for several moments, trying to catch his breath, then chanced a look out of the window. A couple of neighbors were looking over the fence at the shattered drainpipe; but then they just shrugged at each other and turned away, probably thinking it was just an inevitable result of their neighbor's lack of care for his house.

Pat watched them go, then ducked back under the curtains into the darkened room.

And froze.

Before him was a ghost. White skin, white hair, pink eyes.

A female ghost pointing a bony white finger at him.

"Who the hell are you?" it demanded.

But Pat hardly heard.

He was too busy screaming.

Eleven

After a hurried conference in the playground, it was decided that rather than wait for an ambulance, Mr. Smithins himself would drive Eddie and Ivan to the Royal Victoria Hospital for a precautionary checkup. There were few obvious signs of injury: perhaps their faces were a little black, they had a few scratches from scrambling out of the broken window, and when Miss Danvers asked how they were feeling Eddie coughed rather dramatically, but in truth he felt great.

Despite this they were wrapped in blankets—although it was a pleasant afternoon—and rushed to Smithins' car. He drove exactly on the speed limit across the city while Eddie and Ivan sat in the back. Eddie was doing his best not to grin. He felt great. He was a hero. Mr. Smithins had said it, right there in front of practically the entire school.

He could have told them he was a hero already, what with all the baby-snatchers stuff, but this was like doing it in front of a real live audience; he didn't have to tell them anything. They'd seen it with their own eyes. He *was* a hero. The only boy who hadn't seen it with his own eyes was sitting beside him. Ivan, with his sunglasses still firmly in place, looked like he was staring straight ahead. But of course he wasn't. He wasn't staring at anything. Neither was he saying anything. *Perhaps he's in shock*, Eddie thought.

"Are you okay?" Eddie whispered.

"Yes, of course I'm okay," Ivan snapped back. Then he leaned forward to speak to Smithins. "Have my parents been called?"

"Yes, son, they're going to meet us at the hospital."

Ivan nodded and sat back. He turned to Eddie and looked at him for several long moments. Or didn't look at him. Eddie found it quite disconcerting. "When my parents arrive," Ivan said in a low, serious voice, "you tell them we helped each other out. You tell them we're both heroes."

Eddie shrugged.

"Okay?"

Eddie nodded.

"Okay?"

And then he realized what he was doing and said, "Yeah, sure, whatever." Where was the gratitude? Where was the thanks? Hadn't he saved Ivan's life?

"And there's no need to look so smug. You didn't do much."

Eddie was about to snap something back, but then stopped himself. "How can you tell I look so smug?"

"I can't, you dummy—I'm blind. But you sound it. Don't you know that about blind people? When they lose their sight their other senses improve. Like *Daredevil*. Did you see that movie?"

"Sure. Did you?"

"How could I, you dummy, I'm blind."

Eddie sighed. "I saved your life, you can stop calling me dummy."

"You didn't save my life. I could have smashed that window myself. I was just confused for a moment. And don't you forget it."

Eddie shrugged.

"Okay?"

"Yeah. Right." Eddie folded his arms. The ungrateful *sod*.

Smithins, who seemed not to have heard any of this whispered exchange, glanced back at them and smiled. "Malone—I don't think there'll be any need for that detention today. And I hear you got one with Mr. Short as well."

Eddie started to nod, then said: "Mr. Short?"

"Oh yes, we call him that as well. It's a great joke around the staff room—drives him mad. But we'll sort out his detention as well. You're quite the boy, aren't you? First day at school and you save the son of one of our wealthiest benefactors."

There was something about the way he said *benefactors*

that disconcerted Eddie. Was there a hint of sarcasm? "Oh yeah? Who's that then? Who's your dad?"

Ivan said nothing, but as the eagle-faced teacher stopped at a set of traffic lights, he looked back at Eddie. "Why—Billy Cutler. You have heard of Billy Cutler?" Eddie shook his head. Smithins turned further in his seat to study Ivan. "Why don't you tell them about your dad, son?"

"Why don't you just concentrate on the driving?" Ivan snapped.

Eddie sat back in surprise. How could he talk to a teacher like that? And more to the point, why was Smithins not responding? Why wasn't he giving him detention or whacking him with a lump of wood like Danvers? Why did he just give a worried-looking smile and then return his attention to the road ahead?

As they started to move again Eddie realized they were just passing Botanic Station—and sure enough, Bacon and Bap were already in position in case he tried to slope home from school early. They had instructed him to get close to Ivan Cutler—and he'd certainly done that. But even though Ivan Cutler was turning out to be a bit of a pain in the neck, there was no way he'd be passing any information on to the Reservoir Pups. In fact, Eddie reckoned he was such a hero now that when he returned to school he wouldn't have any trouble at all in recruiting members for his gang—and then the Reservoir Pups wouldn't find it quite so easy to intimidate him.

Just as Smithins drove past Bacon and Bap, Eddie

suddenly rapped the window loudly. The Reservoir Pups looked up in time to see Eddie giving them two fingers in a v-sign. It wasn't clever, it wasn't smart, but it felt like absolutely the right thing to do. Eddie then sat back, satisfied; it also allowed Bacon and Bap a clear view of Ivan Cutler. Eddie didn't even look back to see the surprised, and then angry look on their faces.

Up yours, Captain Black!

The Casualty Department of the Royal Victoria Hospital was in a constant state of flux. Belfast, like most cities, could be a dangerous place. When Eddie pushed through the swing doors he could see people who'd been shot, people who'd been knocked down by cars, children who'd gotten their fingers crushed in doors, women who'd set their hair on fire by accident—and that was just on the first set of seats. There were dozens of sets and they all seemed to be full. Smithins guided Ivan Cutler down through the waiting area, looking for a seat. Before Eddie could follow them there was a high-pitched shout from the corridor on his left:

"Eddie!"

He didn't have to turn to recognize his mother's voice.

"Eddie! Are you okay!"

"Yes, Mu—"

Before he could finish he was enveloped in her fleshy arms and she began to smother him in kisses. Eddie dodged this way and that to try to avoid them, but she was bigger and stronger and deeply passionate about slobbering all over him.

"*Mum* . . . ," Eddie whispered, his face scarlet, "*please* . . ."

"Eddie—my hero! That's what they said!"

"*Mum* . . ."

Finally she let him go. She clapped her hands together. She looked really proud. Somehow she'd never seemed quite convinced by his performance against the baby-snatchers, but this was something different. She'd been phoned by the headmaster of the exclusive Brown's Academy himself; he'd described Eddie as a shining example of a young Belfast boy willing to sacrifice himself to save a poor disabled lad, a lad whose parents had, inciden tally, paid for the very science block which had now— thank the Lord—been saved by the fire brigade.

"Eddie—I knew Brown's would be so good for you! You've only been there one day and already it's changed you so much for the better . . ."

"Mum, I would have done it any—"

"It'll be the making of you! Oh, I'm so proud. Are you okay? Have the nurses seen you? Let me take a look at you! Is your throat sore?"

"I'm *fine*. They just brought me as a precaution."

Swing doors opened behind his mum, and Scuttles appeared. He gave Eddie a quick once-over. "Doesn't look too damaged," he said.

His mum shook her head vigorously. "You can never be too sure, we need a doctor to see him—I'll go and see if I can drum one up—one advantage of working in a hospital, eh? At least I can jump the queue." She hurried away, leaving Eddie, for the moment, alone with Scuttles.

"So," Scuttles hissed, "you're the big hero now."

Eddie shrugged.

"Mind you, if I was the headmaster, or the fire brigade, or the police, I'd be asking myself, well, how did that fire start? That's what I'd be asking."

Eddie smiled as pleasantly as he could. "Well," he said, "if you were the headmaster, or the fire brigade or the police, then I might take your question seriously. But seeing as how you're just a big fat cretin in a crap uniform, I don't think I'll bother."

Eddie hurried away down through casualty before Scuttles could respond, or, indeed, slap him in the chops.

He hated Scuttles. He always had, and he always would.

At first Eddie couldn't locate either Ivan Cutler or Smithins anywhere in the waiting area, but then he caught a glimpse of a purple uniform as a nurse approached a curtained-off bed inside the main treatment area. Eddie poked his head through the plastic curtain and saw Ivan sitting on the side of a bed with a doctor listening to his chest through a stethoscope and a nurse standing by taking notes. Obviously Smithins or Ivan knew how to jump a queue as well. Smithins himself was sitting in a plastic chair looking pensive. He managed a smile when Eddie peered in.

"Come on in, Malone—may as well check you out as well."

"My mother—"

"Never mind that—Cutler here's a private patient, no joining the queue for him. You don't mind running the old microscope over this boy as well, do you, Doctor?"

"Stethoscope," said the doctor. "And I really shouldn't—"

"Nonsense!" came a rough bark from the other end of the bed. They all turned to find a tall, heavily muscled man with a thick mustache standing in another gap in the curtains. He had a flat boxer's nose and thick, moist lips, like he'd just finished drinking a pint of beer and eating six hot dogs. He stepped quickly along the length of the bed, his hand dipping into and then out of the inside pocket of his knee-length leather coat. He pressed a fistful of crushed ten-pound notes into the top pocket of the doctor's white housecoat. "You sort him out, eh, Doc? He is a hero after all, isn't he?"

The tall man beamed down at Eddie. He had a gold chain around his neck, a silver bracelet on his wrist and several large and expensive-looking rings on his fingers. "You must be Malone—you saved my boy."

Eddie began to nod, and then remembered himself. "No . . . I . . . we . . . saved each other. . . ."

"Nonsense!" boomed the man, who appeared to be Ivan's dad. "Had it from the headmaster himself. Well done, son."

And he clapped his hand down hard on Eddie's shoulder.

Eddie looked helplessly at Ivan, who looked like thunder.

Ivan's dad then moved along the bed and gave his son every bit as big a hug as Eddie's mum had given him. And it was just about as welcome.

"Are you all right, son, are you okay?" he asked, his voice full of concern.

"Sure," Ivan said coldly, "although there seems to be something wrong with my eyes."

Mr. Cutler looked sort of hurt for a moment, but then

abruptly let loose with a loud, booming laugh. "My boy—always something bright to say, eh!" He turned back to Eddie and punched him playfully on the arm—although with enough strength to create a bruise that Eddie would find later. "You did a good job, kid. Most other boys would have left him where he was, 'cause he's such a smart-arse." He nodded back at his son. "You probably set fire to the school just for fun, didn't you, son?"

"I never—"

"Yeah, yeah, I believe you." He turned and punched Eddie again. Different arm, same sort of bruise. "Tell you what—you come out to the house on Wednesday, see if we can sort you out with some sort of reward."

"Really, there's no—"

"Nonsense! Every need! You saved my boy! Anyone who saves my boy, well, they're a pal of mine, and when you're a pal of mine, you get the best of everything."

He delved into his coat again and produced another ten-pound note. He pushed it into Eddie's blazer pocket and winked. "That'll do for now—come up to the house on Wednesday, I'll sort you out properly. It's my boy's birthday party, we'll have a ball."

Before Eddie could respond his mother appeared through the gap in the curtains Mr. Cutler had left. "Oh, there you are, Eddie, been looking everywhere!" She glanced up at Mr. Cutler, and her mouth dropped open a little bit. There was a clear look of recognition in her eyes. "Ah . . . Eddie . . . come on then . . . I have a doctor. . . ."

"It's all right, Mrs. Malone, we have one lined up

here . . . ," Mr. Cutler said, nodding at the other doctor, who was now busy sounding out Ivan's back.

But Eddie's mum was already leading him away. "No . . . no . . . ," she said, her voice a little quivery, "it's quite all right . . . but thank you . . . thank you. . . ."

She drew the curtain back behind them, and led Eddie away across the ward.

"What's got into you?" said Eddie, annoyed that his mum had stopped him from finding out more about the larger reward his new best pal had promised.

"That man," said his mum.

"Who—Mr. Cutler?"

His mum glanced back at the closed curtains and shook her head. "*Mister*, is it? I don't think so."

"What do you mean? Why, is he a lord or something? I know he paid for the science block at the school."

"Paid for it? Yeah—but what with? No, Eddie. He's no lord. Do you not recognize him from the papers?"

Eddie didn't read the papers. He shook his head.

"Do you not remember him from the news?"

Eddie didn't watch the news. He sighed. Last time his mum had rattled on about him not recognizing someone it had been Alison Beech, leader of the baby-snatchers, and look at the trouble that had led to. . . .

"Eddie—do you *really* not know who that is?"

"Sure I do. He's my new best friend." Eddie was feeling the ten pounds in his pocket and already thinking what he could do with it. He didn't like Ivan Cutler much—but his dad was altogether a different kettle of fish.

"Oh, *Eddie*," his mum said with her familiar, disappointed tone, "don't say *that*."

Eddie sighed. "No, Mum, I don't know who he is, and as a matter of fact I don't particularly—"

"That's Scarface Cutler."

"Who?"

"Eddie—Scarface Cutler. He's the most violent, vicious criminal in the whole city."

"What?" Eddie almost laughed, but there was no trace of mirth on his mother's face. She looked dead serious. Eddie glanced back up the ward. "Him? Are you *sure*?"

"Of course I'm sure. Scarface Cutler."

"But . . . he hasn't got a scar on his face."

His mum rolled her eyes. "Eddie, for goodness' sake. It's not because *he* has a scar on *his* face. It's because he gives *other* people scars on *their* faces."

Eddie swallowed.

He should have guessed.

Finally he met someone who wanted to lavish money and presents on him, and he turned out to be the most violent, vicious criminal in the city.

Scarface Cutler.

Great.

Twelve

Of course, all he had to do was say no.

No.

Simple. Really.

No, I don't want to go to his party. No, I don't want another reward, I did what any right-minded boy would do. I helped a poor blind kid escape from a fire. Yes, I'm great, yes, I'm a hero, but no, I don't want or need to be his friend, I don't want or need to go to his house for a birthday party, I don't want or need to get to know his father—Scarface!— any better than I do already. I appreciate your interest, but no thanks. I'll stay home with Mum and Dad. Or just Mum. Or just Mum and Scuttles. Eddie had been in enough trouble since arriving in Belfast. He didn't need to actively invite any more, and that was surely what he'd be doing if he tried to strike up any sort of a relationship with any members of the Cutler family.

So forget about Ivan Cutler. Forget about Scarface Cutler.

And forget about Captain Black. It was clear to Eddie that Black wasn't interested in Ivan Cutler at all, but in his father, the gangster.

But why?

No, I'm not even thinking about it!

Even though Eddie lived about a hundred meters from the hospital, his mum insisted that Scuttles went and got his car and drove them both home. Scuttles scowled at him as he drove, particularly when Eddie made low groaning noises from the backseat, just to wind him up. Scuttles went back to work, muttering to himself, while Eddie's mum took him up to the apartment and tucked him into bed.

"Mum, I really don't think I need to—"

"Shhhh, and I'll get you a hot-water bottle. . . ."

"Mum, I don't need a—"

"And a nice cup of hot milk . . ."

"Mum, for goodness' sake, I'm—"

"You're a hero," she said, hugging him suddenly, "and you're the only boy I have in the world and I might have lost you and I'm going to get you hot milk and a hot-water bottle and you can even have some Jaffa . . . I mean some nice biscuits . . ." She kissed him on the forehead and then the cheek and then scurried away.

Eddie lay back in bed, lifted the remote for the portable TV and switched it on. They still didn't have cable, but luckily *The Simpsons* was on BBC 2. Mum didn't like him watching *The Simpsons* because she thought the characters were far too cheeky, but she would make an exception today, for her hero. After ten minutes Eddie sat up in bed again and sighed. He didn't particularly want hot milk, biscuits or a hot-water bottle, but she was still taking an awful long time bringing them.

As if she had been listening in on his thoughts, the door opened a moment later and in she came carrying a tray with the milk and biscuits. The hot-water bottle was wedged under her arm.

"Here we go . . . ," she said, setting the tray on his lap. "Sorry I was so long, but you had visitors."

"I had . . . ?"

"But not this evening, young man—you need your rest. . . ."

"Mum . . . who was it?"

"Oh—just that silly little girl with the white hair—"

"Mum!"

Eddie quickly moved the tray to one side and threw the quilt back. Mo was back!

"Just you stay exactly where you are, young man!"

Eddie pulled his bathrobe on over his pajamas.

"Don't you move an inch!"

Eddie checked his reflection in the dressing table mirror and smoothed his hair down.

"I am ordering you to get back into that bed!"

Eddie turned for the door.

"Eddie Malone!"

"Mum—I'm fine, the doctor says I'm fine, I'll be five minutes."

His mum sighed. "No longer."

"I swear to God. No longer than ten."

"Eddie—"

But he was already pulling the front door open.

He hurried out into the hall—but there was no sign of her.

"Mo!"

Eddie charged toward the lifts.

"Mo!"

He rounded the corner. "Mo! M—"

"What are you so excited about?"

Eddie turned to his right. She was standing by the wall on the far side of the elevators where you could look out over the hospital. Same white hair tucked up under a baseball cap. Same pink eyes and deathly pale complexion. Same superior look. Same upright stance that made her look like she was about to throw a punch or start a riot. All the things that would normally have annoyed him in a girl, or, indeed, a boy, but in Mo somehow it . . . didn't.

"Mo!" Eddie said, and realized immediately that his voice was rather higher than normal. "MO," he repeated, but lower, deeper, gruffer. "What're you . . . how did you . . . why are you . . . Mo?"

She gave him half a smile. "Yeah. Missed you too."

"I mean," Eddie said, clearing his throat and trying to regain control of the situation, "I mean, we were supposed to be a gang. Then I call round and your dad says you've moved to Scotland. Like, thanks for telling me."

"I couldn't, Eddie. There wasn't time."

"No phone call, no e-mail."

"It wasn't possible."

"Yeah, right."

"Eddie, I'm here now, so are you going to be obnoxious or are we going to get on with it?"

"I'll be whatever I want to . . . get on with what?"

"Our mission."

"What mission?"

"To reclaim the head of Oliver Plunkett."

Eddie nodded to himself for several moments. Then he said: "What are you talking about? Who is Oliver Plunkett? Who gave you the right to decide that we had a mission at all? And who says you can just call out of nowhere after disappearing like that? Without a word of explanation or an apology or, or . . ."

Mo folded her arms and shook her head. "Why, Eddie," she said, "anyone would think you were in love with me."

Eddie blushed immediately and cursed to himself at the same time, because he was aware that he was blushing and couldn't do a thing about it.

He was one of life's blushers.

There are people who don't, and people who do.

Sometimes blushing can be quite nice—it's a highly visible way of revealing your innermost feelings. You meet a nice girl, or a football hero, or a movie star and you blush because it shows what high regard you hold that girl or footballer or actor in. It's cute. But it can also be horrible. Someone can shout, who stole my handbag?—and you blush and look guilty, even though you had nothing to do with it. Someone can shout, hands up who likes wearing dresses, to a gang of boys, and you won't put your hand up but you'll blush, even though you've no interest in dresses, but everyone will think you're a secret girly. And if some important army general rushes into the United Nations and yells that someone has stolen a nuclear bomb and is about to start World War Three, you'll blush, you'll be arrested and then executed, even though you had nothing to do with stealing the bomb at all.

So Eddie blushed, even though he didn't love Mo, or at least hadn't even thought about whether he loved, or even liked, Mo.

"Don't talk rubbish," Eddie snapped, and coughed in an exaggerated fashion, which would make anyone's face red. "Sorry," he said, "my throat . . . I was in a fire . . . at the school . . . I saved . . ." He folded his arms and pushed his chin out and said: "So stop talking crap and tell me where you've been."

"I haven't been anywhere," said Mo.

"Right. Sure. Listen, I called round to your house. Your dad said you'd gone to Scotland."

"Well, he would say that, wouldn't he?"

"What are you talking about?"

"Well, he doesn't know you from Adam. He wasn't going to tell you where I really was."

"Why not?"

Mo sighed. "Because, numbskull, he's just out of prison for shooting someone, he drinks, he hasn't got a job, the Social Services came round and said he wasn't allowed to look after me until they decide whether he's capable of it, they insisted that I went to stay with my relatives in Scotland. They even bought me a ticket. Except I didn't go. I'm not going to bloody Scotland. He's my dad, he might be hard work, but he's still my dad. So I've been hiding out in the house. I haven't been going out. We keep the blinds closed. That's why I couldn't come to our meetings." She shrugged. "Sorry," she said.

"You mean you were there when I called."

"Yes, course I was."

Eddie finally managed a smile. The blush had died down by now. "So you've got it all sorted out now, you're allowed to live with your dad."

Mo shook her head. "No, Eddie, if the Social Services find out I'm still here they'll throw my da back in prison and me into a children's home."

"So what are you doing *here*?"

"Because we've got to find the head of Oliver Plunkett."

"And for the last time, who the hell is Oliver Plunkett?"

A different voice came from behind Eddie. "He's a saint and a scholar."

Eddie spun—fearing it was some kind of trap—and found a boy of roughly his age, wearing jeans, a T-shirt, an anorak and a determined expression. He looked kind of grubby and tired, but also quite tough.

"And who the hell are you?" Eddie demanded.

"This is Pat," said Mo. "He's on a mission from God."

Mo asked Pat to remain where he was, then led Eddie back down the hall toward his apartment.

"What are you like?" she whispered.

"What are you talking about now?"

"I've spent the last couple of hours reassuring Pat that

you can be trusted, that you're the rough tough leader of the most dangerous gang in the city, and you come out wearing bunny slippers."

She nodded down at his feet. Eddie's mouth dropped open a fraction while he floundered around for something to say, some kind of response that would explain or excuse the fact that he was indeed wearing . . . bunny slippers.

At least they weren't pink.

They were blue.

For boys.

Little boys.

"They're . . . not mine. . . ."

"Yeah, right."

"Anyway . . . they could be . . . evil bunnies."

"Please stop, Eddie, you're not making things any better. Just—get rid."

Eddie took them off—and threw them over the side of the wall. They fell to their deaths seventeen floors below. They were a Christmas present from his mum. He had always hated them with a passion—but sometimes it was cold in the mornings, and they were quite comfortable.

"Okay. There you go. Now can you tell me what's going on? Who is he? I don't like him."

"You don't know him, Eddie."

"What does he want?"

"He doesn't *want* anything. But he needs our help, though he won't admit that."

"Our help for what? You're talking in circles. Just tell me what's going on, Mo."

So she told him about finding the boy in her room, about the fact that he was on the run from an orphanage south of the border, about the fact that he was in pursuit of the head of Oliver Plunkett. She said, don't you ever watch the news? And he said no. She told him who Oliver Plunkett was, that his head was magically preserved, that if the primate was going to become pope then they had to get the head back to Drogheda before the current pope arrived in four days.

Eddie nodded thoughtfully. "And you're not making this up?"

"No!"

He glanced back at Pat.

"And you're sure he's not making it up?"

"Yes!"

"And if you're not, and he's not, and the head of Oliver Plunkett has been stolen, why the hell should I care whether it turns up or not? Who gives a damn about whether some primate becomes the next pope or not? Anyway, I thought primates were monkeys."

"Don't be thick, Eddie."

"Okay," said Eddie. He wasn't being thick, he was trying to be smart. And failing. He glanced back at Pat again. He didn't look the most friendly boy in the world. But then if he really was on the run from an orphanage, if he really had been sent on a mission by God, then Eddie was sure *he* wouldn't look particularly cheerful either. "Then answer my question. Why should I care?"

"Because he needs our help."

"Not good enough."

"Because the future of the Catholic church in Ireland rests on it."

"Not good enough."

"Because the head is worth three million euros."

"Now you're talking."

Eddie smiled, Mo smiled, and together they looked back to Pat and smiled at him and gave him the thumbs-up.

Pat hesitated for a moment, then raised a thumb as well.

"Three million euros, you say," Eddie whispered.

"At the very least," Mo whispered back.

Thirteen

Eddie lay fully dressed beneath his quilt while his mum finished kissing—well, slobbering all over—Scuttles. He wanted to jump up and batter Scuttles with a frozen turkey, but he had to be strong. He had to lie there and listen to the smack-smack-gush-gush of their lips because there was three million euros at stake.

At *least* three million euros.

At some point his mum reclaimed her lips; then he had to endure listening to them argue playfully. Scuttles was pleading to be allowed to stay; and Mum was saying of course he could—as soon as he was divorced from his wife. Eventually Scuttles moaned off into the night. Eddie then heard his mum rifling through the kitchen cupboards. He knew what she was up to. She was looking for the packet of Jaffa cakes she'd hidden from him. She wasn't aware that he'd found it, and eaten it, in three minutes, seventeen seconds. After a while she gave up and retired to the bathroom where she removed her makeup and brushed her hair while singing "I Lost My Heart to a Starship Trooper" in a rather quavery voice. He closed his eyes and pretended to be asleep when she opened the door and softly called his name; then he heard her blow him a kiss and close the door. She was on the early shift the next morning, and so she was retiring well before her normal time. Eventually, eventually he heard the click of her bedside lamp. He lay impatiently for a further forty-five minutes until the BOOM BOOM BOOM of her snores—and the gentle vibration of the building— confirmed that she was well and truly asleep. At last he was able to slip out of the apartment and join Mo and the new boy, Pat, downstairs.

It was a little after ten o'clock, and now that September had rolled around again, already dark. They skirted the edge of the Rivers, their eyes peeled for Reservoir Pups, and then entered another estate, this one ruled by the widely feared Andytown Albinos. Only Eddie and Scuttles knew that in fact there was just one Andytown Albino.

Mo.

She continued to fool most of the people, most of the time.

Most importantly, Captain Black and the Reservoir Pups still believed that the AAs were a huge and fearsome gang.

So it was with a sigh of relief that Eddie entered

Andytown and walked with Mo and Pat toward her father's house safe in the knowledge that at least they weren't going to be attacked *here*.

"You sure you're all right about this?" Eddie asked as they walked. It was a difficult thing, asking a daughter to spy on her dad. But there was no alternative. He was the one connection they had to the head of Oliver Plunkett.

"Of course I'm sure," Mo said, although Eddie wasn't convinced. At first, when Pat had told him why he'd targeted Mo's dad Eddie had laughed and said, "That's the best you have?" and they'd almost come to blows over it; but then Mo had said that actually she thought Pat had the right idea. Her dad had even told her that the car had been stolen—but if it had been stolen, then how come he suddenly had several hundred pounds in his wallet? She knew this for a fact. Because she'd stolen twenty earlier. And how come, after weeks of his refusing to have anything to do with the men who'd helped get him sent to prison, they'd suddenly appeared on his doorstep one night? And how come her dad, who liked to think he was rough and tough, had been so scared when he came back into the house, shaking and panting and sweating—and then refused to talk to her about it?

It was clear to Mo what had happened. "Those guys—they threatened him, ordered him to sell them the car for a couple of hundred pounds—and then made him report it stolen, but not until after they'd used it."

Pat nodded enthusiastically.

"But what . . . what if your dad's actually part of it?" Eddie asked. "What if he stole the head?"

Mo sucked at one of her lips, then shook her head. "No. He wouldn't do that. I'm sure he wouldn't do that. He sold the car because they forced him to. And because he doesn't have enough money to look after me. That's all."

Eddie nodded and kept walking. But he knew her dad didn't have a job, and if the Social Services thought she was living in Scotland, they wouldn't be paying him any child support either. So money was tight. That was a good enough reason to sell the car—or indeed, to steal the head.

He hadn't liked Mo's dad when he met him. He looked mean, he acted mean, he said mean things. In Eddie's book that added up to him being, well, mean. It didn't make him a head-snatcher, but neither did it make him . . . not a head-snatcher.

Eventually they took up a position at the end of Mo's street, hiding by the back wall of the long-closed shop where Pat had stood earlier. It allowed them to cover both the main street, and the alley behind.

"Every night, as soon as he checks I'm asleep," Mo was saying, "he goes out. Next morning he stinks of beer. So you don't have to be Basil the Great Mouse Detective to work out he goes to the pub. His usual one's just around the corner, so we follow him, see who he meets. It's a long shot, but . . ."

Eddie nodded. "But you're out here with us—how's he going to check you're asleep?"

Mo rolled her eyes. "I'm going in now, numbskull. Normally I climb up and down the pipe at the back—but some clot broke it trying to break into my house." She gave Pat an evil look, but then softened it with a smile.

"Sorry," he said.

"Never worry," said Mo, "I have other ways."

Mo slipped away down the alley toward her house, leaving Eddie and Pat standing somewhat awkwardly in the dark.

Eddie had lots of interesting questions he wanted to ask Pat—like, what happened to your mum and dad, was their car accident really horrific? Did you see their dead bodies? Did their heads come off? What's an orphanage like? Do they beat you with sticks? Do they make you take baths in boiling water? Or freezing water? Are you all too horrible to be adopted? Is it really smelly? Are the girls really ugly? Are you all covered in nits and fleas and boils? But, he supposed, correctly, that these questions might cause offense. So he went for something that couldn't possibly rub his new ally up the wrong way.

"What football team do you support?"

"Celtic," said Pat. "You?"

"Rangers."

They nodded warily at each other. Both teams were Scottish, and operated out of the same city, Glasgow. That was about all they had in common. Rangers fans hated Celtic fans. Celtic fans hated Rangers fans. It didn't really have anything to do with football. It had to do with religion and politics, as most things that end in violence usually do. Eddie wasn't even that interested in football, it was just something that he'd grown up with, like preferring chips to mashed potatoes, burgers to steak. Rangers to Celtic. *Change the subject*, thought Eddie.

"So Mo says your parents died in a horrific car crash."

"Mo says your dad's run off with a doctor."

Eddie looked down the alley.

Pat looked down the street.

"You don't really believe all that crap about the head, do you?" Eddie asked. "That it's miraculously preserved. That it can do magic tricks."

"I never said it could do tricks," said Pat.

"Good.We agree on something."

"I said it could do miracles. Different thing entirely."

Eddie sighed. "It's only an old head," he said.

"It's a saint's head, thousands of people come to visit it every year."

Eddie shrugged. "Thousands of people visit the circus every year, doesn't mean the monkeys can work miracles."

"No," said Pat, "but they can probably do tricks."

They blinked at each other in the deepening darkness. *Is he trying to be smart? I don't think I like him much.* They were both thinking exactly the same things.

"You don't really think you're on a mission from God, do you?" Eddie asked.

Pat shrugged.

"And what do you care who the next pope is? You'll still be stuck in an orphanage."

Pat shrugged again. Then he said, hesitantly, "Because it's the right thing to do."

Eddie would have snapped something smart back—but he couldn't think of anything. *The right thing to do?* Eddie was in it for the money and the glory. That seemed just about right to him. But there was something about the innocent way that Pat had said it that made Eddie feel quite . . .

Pat suddenly grabbed Eddie by the arm and pulled him, off balance, into the darkest part of the shop doorway. "Hey!" Eddie raised his fists defensively, fearing that Pat had decided that violence was the only way to settle their differences—but instead he saw that Pat was pointing away down the street; Eddie turned to see that a car had pulled to a halt several doors short of Mo's house. It rolled forward several feet, stopped, then moved again, as if the driver was looking for a particular house number.

Finally it stopped directly outside Mo's house and a man wearing a crumpled jacket, crumpled trousers and a crumpled shirt climbed out.

"Crumples," Pat said under his breath.

"What?" Eddie whispered.

"Not what. Who. He's a reporter. He's been following me around."

This wasn't strictly the truth.

"Well, what's he doing here?"

Pat shrugged, although it was perfectly obvious what he was doing. He was looking for Oliver Plunkett's head. Crumples approached the front door, peered through a window, and then knocked. Mo's dad answered. They couldn't hear what was being said. There is a phrase which is quite appropriate here: actions speak louder than words.

Mo's dad grabbed Crumples by the lapels and threw him across the pavement. He hit the hood of his car and rolled up and over it before disappearing over the other side. It was several long moments before an even more crumpled-looking Crumples slowly raised himself above the hood and peered nervously back toward Mo's dad, who was standing with his hands bunched up into fists, breathing hard, looking tough.

"I take it that's a no?" Crumples shouted, loud enough now for Pat and Eddie to hear.

Mo's dad snarled and stepped forward like a tiger ready to pounce . . . albeit, a big fat tiger in a stained vest. But before he got anywhere near the reporter, Crumples jumped into his car and drove off at speed.

Mo's dad disappeared back inside the house—but left the door open. A few minutes later he reappeared, now wearing a shirt over his vest and zipping shut a black jacket. He glanced back up the stairs behind him, then closed the door gently and began to walk up the street toward them. Eddie and Pat backed up hard against the shop door and waited for him to pass. They sucked in their chests and tried not to breathe as he stopped just a couple of feet away and checked his jacket for cigarettes. He found a box, took one out with his mouth, then produced a lighter and clicked it unsuccessfully several times, until the flame caught. If he'd been looking the right way he would have seen Eddie and Pat. But he wasn't, and he didn't. He blew out a stream of smoke and hurried on.

Then Mo jogged up.

"What was that all about?" said Pat. "What did the journalist want?"

"You know him?"

"Sure," said Pat, "that's the fella I met on the train."

He didn't mention that he'd stolen a hundred and fifty euros from him. Or that he'd whacked him in the willy.

Mo glanced at Eddie. "He said he knew my dad was involved in the theft of the head."

"God," said Eddie. "What'd your dad say?"

"He said if he ever came round here again he'd break his neck. And then he nearly did."

They turned then and followed Mo's dad to the pub. Except he didn't stop there. He walked right on past the Brewer's Drip. Mo shrugged helplessly and they continued after him. The streets hereabouts were long and straight, which should have made it difficult for them to follow him undetected, but most of the streetlights had been broken over the years by kids throwing stones, and had never been replaced, so it was dark enough for them to follow him relatively closely without being noticed.

He walked for about half a mile, stopping occasionally to light another cigarette. Eventually he approached a long, low building which had a sign in bright green letters hanging above its doors: ANDYTOWN CELTIC SUPPORTERS CLUB. The windows were festooned with green and white pennants; there was a green and white flag fluttering from a pole jutting out from the side of the building. The window ledges were painted green, the plastic guttering outside was green; the very walls were green. The only thing that wasn't green was the suit the bouncer in the doorway was wearing; it was black as a funeral; he wore a black shirt as well and sharp, black and pointy winkle-picker boots. Mo's dad walked up and spoke briefly to him; then he raised his hands and was searched for weapons.

They crouched down behind a car and watched as Mo's

dad was given the all-clear by the bouncer and entered the club.

"What now?" said Eddie.

"We have to go in," said Pat. "We have to find out who he's talking to. That journalist probably spooked him, he's going to report it to someone."

"Or, alternatively," said Eddie, "we wait here and see who he comes out with."

Pat nodded. "I see. That would be the chicken way, I believe."

"The *what*?" Eddie snapped.

"The big chicken way."

"The *what*?" Eddie snapped again.

"Okay," said Mo, sensing that fists might start flying at any moment, "calm down. You both have a point. But it's my dad, it should be my—"

"Holy *crap*!" Eddie exclaimed suddenly. Mo's head jerked toward him, ready to start the fighting herself this time, but then she saw that he wasn't even looking at her, but back across the road to the club, and at the sleek green Porsche sports car that had pulled to a halt outside it. The bouncer, suddenly smiling widely, hurried up to the driver's door and opened it. A tall, heavily muscled man with a thick mustache and a flat boxer's nose climbed out. He was wearing an expensive-looking but also very bright green suit. As he shook the hand of the bouncer the lights from the club reflected off the silver bracelet on his right wrist and the chunky gold chain around his neck.

"What, Eddie? What is it?" Mo was saying.

"Not what . . . *who* . . . ," Eddie said vaguely.

"Who then?" said Mo.

Eddie slumped back down behind the car, shaking his head. He looked at Pat. "Okay," he said, "you win."

Pat smiled. "We are going in, then?" he said.

"No," said Eddie, "you were right. I am a big fat chicken. There's no way on earth I'm going in there after Scarface Cutler."

Fourteen

Eddie, who'd only known for a couple of hours himself who Scarface Cutler was, explained to Pat and Mo in as much horrific detail as he could manage exactly who the large man in the green suit was, and why it would be madness to even contemplate gaining entry to the Andytown Celtic Supporters Club. They listened attentively, and made the appropriate faces when he described how Scarface sliced his victims from ear to ear.

When he'd finished they sat quietly thinking about their situation in the cool night air. There were vague sounds drifting across from the bar of the Celtic Supporters Club: the dull beat of a jukebox, the clink of glasses, somebody being sick in the toilets.

Finally Pat raised himself. He crept forward and stared through the car windows at the club and the bouncer standing outside it. "I don't care who this Scarface is," he said, "but I'm going in. I have to find the head. I'm on a mission from—"

"We *know*," Eddie said under his breath. He turned to Mo for support.

But it was not forthcoming.

"I'm going too, Eddie," she said. "My dad's in there, I was going in anyway, but if Scarface Cutler is as dangerous as you say he is, then I'm definitely going in. I have to make sure my dad's okay. Okay?"

But it wasn't okay.

Eddie fumed.

He had dreamt of world domination, and now he wasn't even dominating these two kids.

If he was ever going to become a benevolent world leader, or indeed a power-crazed dictator, he would have to start somewhere. He would have to start *now*.

"No," he said firmly, "as a matter of fact—it's not okay. And you're not going."

They looked at him as if he'd suddenly grown two heads.

"What?" said Mo.

"I said, you're not going. And neither are you." He nodded at Pat.

"I'd like to see you try and stop me," Pat hissed. He raised himself up further behind the car. Mo rose with him.

"Look," Eddie snapped, "either I'm the leader of this gang or I'm not."

He wasn't sure what reaction he expected, although he would have settled for them dropping to their knees and worshipping him. But they didn't. Instead Mo glanced coolly back at him and said: "Okay. You're not."

She returned her attention to the club across the road.

Eddie sighed. He had to do *something*. He couldn't just sit there on the damp footpath and let them go ahead and try to enter the club. It wasn't because he was scared. He was—but that wasn't the main reason. It was because they didn't have a plan. They were just going to blunder in there and hope that things worked out. Maybe they would get lucky—or maybe they would be discovered and beaten to a pulp. And Mo was wrong. He *was* a leader. He was a leader of a gang with no name, and possibly no members. But it was still his gang and he would show them that he was its natural leader, not by force, not by brutality or harsh discipline, not by buying their loyalty. But by common sense.

"Look—" he began.

"Shhhhh," said Mo.

"I need to explain—"

"Will you shut up?" Pat hissed back.

"NO I WILL NOT!" Eddie grabbed Pat by the back of the neck and squeezed hard, forcing him back down onto the ground.

"Eddie!" said Mo, then glanced fearfully back in the direction of the bouncer, who was now looking their way. She ducked down quickly. "What are you doing?"

"You put one finger on me again . . . !" Pat warned, raising his fist.

"Just . . . *listen*, then."

Eddie said it with terrific intensity, his eyes as wide as

his nostrils were flared, his brow furrowed with concentration, his cheeks flushed not with embarrassment but with concern. Mo had never seen him like this before. She was angry that he was speaking to her like this—but also quite impressed. She put a hand on Pat's leg. "Let him speak," she said.

Pat glared at Eddie for a further few seconds, then reluctantly nodded.

"Okay. Okay. Right." This was his big moment. "Look," he said, "sometimes you've got to look at the bigger picture." Then he hesitated as he tried to conjure up the words to match the ideas that were slowly forming in his brain. "Okay—okay. Pat, I appreciate how desperate you are to get the head back, and you've done really well to get this far—but if you go blundering in there the chances are you'll get caught and end up beaten up or dead or both, and that's not going to get you the head back. And Mo, I know how concerned you are for your dad—but he's gone in there of his own free will. If he was scared of someone he wouldn't just walk in there. The chances are he's gone in there for a reason—probably to tell whoever's involved in the theft of the head that there's a journalist on his tail."

"Eddie—I understand that. But how are we ever going to know if we don't go in and listen?"

"They might be discussing the head right now," said Pat, "and we're missing it."

"I know, I know," said Eddie, "we probably are—but I'm telling you, it's a small club, there's bouncers, the chances of us getting close enough to hear are tiny. Mo, there isn't always a handy tunnel or secret entrance, sometimes you just have to admit that there's no safe way of doing it."

"Well, what do we do then?" said Mo. "Just give up without trying?"

"No," said Eddie. "We look at the evidence. Mo—your dad sells a car to some local gangsters, then panics when a journalist comes to call. So he goes to that club to tell the gangsters about it, and at the same time Scarface Cutler arrives. Scarface is a major-league gangster. The chances are, therefore, that he's responsible for the theft of the head. But he's not going to carry it around with him in the back of his Porsche, is he? What we need to do is search his house."

"Just like that?" said Mo.

"Yeah, what're we gonna do, just walk up and ring his doorbell?"

And Eddie surprised them both by nodding.

Eddie told them all about saving Ivan Cutler's life and his subsequent invitation to the blind boy's birthday party. They thought it was a remarkable coincidence that the party he was invited to should just happen to be at a house owned by their new chief suspect for the theft of the head of Saint Oliver Plunkett, but they accepted that life was sometimes like that. Eddie chose not to tell them that it was no coincidence at all, that he had been ordered to get to know Ivan Cutler by Captain Black of the Reservoir Pups. They really didn't need to know that at all. Not yet.

But at least they now agreed that any attempt to enter

the Celtic Supporters Club would be folly, and that instead they should focus their attention on the birthday party. It was two days away. The pope was arriving in Ireland in four days' time and going directly to the service in Drogheda Cathedral. They had to have the head back by then or—well, not to be too dramatic about it, Pat would burn in Hell for all eternity.

"Well," Eddie said, "not to be too dramatic about it, I'll also burn in Hell for all eternity if I don't get home." It was now just after midnight. He winked at Mo. "I'll, uh, talk to you two tomorrow."

What he really meant was that he'd talk to Mo tomorrow. She was part of his gang. Pat was just some blow-in from south of the border who would help make them very rich indeed. Eddie turned to begin the long walk back to the nurses' quarters. He'd only gone a few yards when Mo came running up after him. Pat stayed where he was.

"What about Pat?" she asked, keeping her voice low.

"He can hang around with us until we get the head back, but I don't want him in the gang."

"I don't mean that. I mean what about him tonight. Where's he going to sleep?"

"What's it got to do with me?"

"It's got to do with you because you made a big song and dance about being our leader. So you have to look after him."

"I never made a song and dance. And if I am your leader, then I order you to look after him."

Mo shook her head. "I would if I could, Eddie, but I

can't. You know I can't. Dad has enough trouble keeping me secret. Anyway, it would make him suspicious."

"Okay then. I'm sure he can find a park bench or a shop doorway or . . ."

Mo was giving him a *look*.

"No," said Eddie.

"Yes," said Mo.

"No," said Eddie.

Mo folded her arms. Eddie folded his. Mo looked back at Pat. "Pat—Eddie wants you to stay at his place."

Pat didn't look convinced. He nodded at Eddie. Eddie glared once again at Mo, then nodded back. "You owe me," he whispered angrily out of the side of his mouth.

"Not as much as you owe me," Mo whispered just as angrily back.

Fifteen

Getting him into the apartment wasn't the problem. As they traveled up in the lift Pat said, "What's that noise?"

"My mum snoring."

"No, seriously, what's that noise, is there something wrong with the lift?"

"No," Eddie said patiently, "that really is my mum snoring."

When they entered the apartment Pat put his hands to his ears and said: "You really ought to do something about that."

Eddie had grown so used to the volume of his mother's snoring that he hardly noticed it anymore. And in truth it wasn't *that* bad. But he supposed that if Pat lived in an orphanage, and the discipline there was really fierce, then they probably weren't allowed to make a peep after lights-out. Under those circumstances, then his mum's snoring probably did sound tremendously loud.

"Don't worry about it," Eddie said, leading Pat across the lounge and through the kitchen, "you'll get used to it."

He regretted that almost immediately, because it carried with it a suggestion that Pat would be around long enough for him to get used to it. This was strictly a one-night arrangement. Eddie had just a single bed, but there was plenty of room beneath it for Pat to sleep. It wouldn't be very comfortable, but it was better than dossing down in a shop doorway. Eddie opened his bedroom door, and nodded for Pat to enter—but he remained standing in the kitchen.

"Pat . . . ," said Eddie.

But Pat wasn't moving. Instead he nodded at the fridge. "I'm starving," he said.

Eddie rolled his eyes at Pat. Pat rolled them back.

"Just some toast or something."

"My mum will wake up."

But Pat stood his ground. Eddie stomped back into the kitchen and put two slices of bread into the toaster. They stood around, not speaking to each other while they waited for it to pop. When it did, Eddie put the two slices on a plate and handed them to Pat. Pat looked at them.

"What?" said Eddie.

"Well, some butter or jam or both might be nice."

Eddie pulled open the fridge, removed the butter and jam and set them down on the kitchen table. "I presume you can butter toast yourself?" he snapped.

Pat went to work.

Eddie decided to leave him to it. He went to the bathroom and brushed his teeth. He studied his reflection in the mirror; he looked tired, although it was difficult to tell how tired as the mirror was vibrating gently because of his mother's snoring, throwing his reflection slightly out of focus. He yawned. He was being mean to Pat for no particular reason. He seemed to recall being mean to Mo when he'd first met her as well. He rubbed at his brow. He was tired. It was late. He had to go back to school in the morning. What was he supposed to do with Pat then?

Eddie flushed the toilet and returned to the kitchen. This would be the sticky bit, persuading Pat that he had to sleep *under* the bed. Eddie reminded himself not to say, beggars can't be choosers. There would only be another fight. Be nice. Be friendly. But be *firm*.

Except Pat wasn't in the kitchen.

Eddie followed a trail of crumbs down the hall to his bedroom, and then stood with his mouth hanging open in the doorway at the sight of Pat sprawled over the top of his bed, fast asleep, a jammy crust stuck to the pillow by his cheek.

"Brilliant," said Eddie, "just brilliant."

Eddie was curled up in a spare quilt at the bottom of the bed enjoying a really quite pleasant dream when he was torn from his slumbers by an ear-piercing scream. He shot up to find Pat sitting up in his bed, shaking and crying and saying over and over again, "No, don't . . . no, don't . . . no . . . don't . . ." He still had his eyes closed, and was clearly still caught in the grip of a nightmare.

From the next room Eddie's mum called: "Eddie? Are you all right? I thought I heard—"

"Just a dream, Mum . . . go back to sleep."

"Are you sure? Do you want a glass of hot milk?"

"No!"

What was it with hot milk these days?

Eddie looked back to his bed, where Pat had now opened his eyes and was looking around the room with a confused expression. His hair was damp and plastered down against his skull and his eyes were red-rimmed. Dawn was just creeping up outside, slowly transforming the bedroom from black to gray.

"What . . . where?" Pat said vaguely.

"You had a nightmare," said Eddie.

Pat nodded slowly. "The head . . . I saw the head. . . ."

"Well, it's over," said Eddie.

"It was coming toward me, its eyes were open, it was speaking. . . ."

"I get the picture," said Eddie, "now why don't you lie down and—"

"It was saying 'Into Thy Hands O Lord I Commend My Spirit.' . . ." Pat shuddered and lay back. "I thought it was going to kill me."

No, Eddie thought, *I'm going to kill you. Just let me sleep.*

Eddie lay down again and wrapped himself in his quilt. He squinted at his watch in the gloom. It was a little after five. He still had a couple of hours.

"I'm sorry," Pat said quietly.

Eddie lay still for several moments, wondering whether he should just pretend to be asleep. But eventually he said: "What for? Stealing my bed or disturbing my sleep?"

"Both."

"Okay."

Eddie closed his eyes.

"And for just generally being a bit lippy. I'm just nervous. I'm in a strange country. I don't know who I can trust. I have to get the head back."

"Okay," said Eddie.

"You're right about Scarface Cutler. That's the way to go. Go to his party, check out the lie of the land, find out where the head is, steal it back."

"Okay."

"There's still time, I mean, if it's there, and we can get at it, and get away, there's still time, I can catch the train, or take a taxi or—"

"Pat?"

"What?"

"Would you ever shut up and let me sleep?"

"Oh. Right. Okay."

Eddie turned over and closed his eyes.

"Eddie?"

"*What?*"

"Thanks for the toast. And letting me stay."

"Okay."

"I think you'll make a great gang leader."

"Okay."

"Imagine breaking into a church, stealing a saint's sacred head and then trying to ransom it back for three million euros. Those scumbags just want to make money out of Oliver Plunkett's head."

"Scumbags," muttered Eddie, finally drifting off to sleep dreaming about the houses, the speedboats and the fast cars he could buy with three million euros.

Sixteen

Eddie wasn't expecting to be carried shoulder high around the grounds of Brown's Academy when he arrived the next morning, but at the very least he had hoped for a change in attitude from his fellow pupils and the teachers. He was, after all, a hero. You only had to examine the blackened brickwork of the science block to see how serious the fire had been; you only had to peer through the smashed windows at the cracked and melted laboratory equipment to appreciate that Eddie had braved an inferno to save Ivan Cutler. But from the moment he walked through the gates he was ignored; when he tried to start up conversations he was cut off; when he approached groups of boys, they split up and hurried away.

"What's wrong with everyone?" he said aloud.

From behind a familiar voice said: "They don't like Ivan Cutler."

Eddie turned to find Gary Gilmore standing with his hands in his pockets, looking equally friendless. "What's that got to do with anything?"

"They think he's a bully, they think he squeals to the teachers, they think the teachers won't tell him off because his dad's a thug. They hate him."

"Okay, but so what? What's it got to do with me."

"You saved him."

"What was I supposed to do, let him burn?"

Gary shrugged. "They reckon you're his best friend now."

"I hardly know him. And what I know, I don't much like."

"They say you're going to his birthday party."

"How would they know?"

"Are you?"

"I . . . well, I've been invited. Doesn't mean we're best mates."

Gary raised an eyebrow. "Looks like it, though."

Eddie shook his head again. "This is ridiculous. I can't win." He sighed. "Well, at least the teachers will give me an easier time."

Gary shook his head.

"Oh for God's sake," said Eddie, "what?"

"Seems the fire brigade have made their report. Seems they think the fire was started deliberately. Seems they think you and me might have started it."

"*What?*"

"Headmaster had a meeting with the police this morning. Enjoy your second day at Brown's, Eddie, because it might be your last."

"You're serious?"

"I'm always serious."

"But what can we do?"

"What you do is up to you." He moved closer, then dropped his voice. "If they try to expel me," he said, patting a small bulge in his blazer pocket, "then I'm going to blow up the rest of the school as well."

He winked, then hurried away across the playground. Eddie watched as he walked toward the main school building—and then saw a teacher quickly follow him in. Eddie glanced around; across the playground another teacher quickly looked away.

Great, he thought, *now I'm being watched.*

Throughout the morning Eddie found himself under close scrutiny whether he was in class or walking between them. *In* class it was invariably he who was asked questions, he who was asked to read aloud, he who was told to be quiet even if it was the rest of the class that was making noise. Dopey Danvers threatened him twice with the Bloody Hell.

At lunchtime, once again faced with nobody to talk to, Eddie reluctantly approached Ivan Cutler, who was also standing by himself. As he drew near he could see that Ivan was holding his right hand gingerly.

"All right, Ivan?" he said. "What'd you do to your hand?"

"I did nothing," Ivan snapped back. "Danvers did it."

"The Bloody Hell?"

"The Bloody Hell. I'm going to get her back. I swear to God I'm going to get her back. And wait till my dad finds out. He'll have her sacked."

"Why did she hit you?"

"Because I called her a stupid cow."

Eddie cleared his throat.

After lunch he had three more classes—geography, history and math. On his way to math somebody tripped him from behind and he went sprawling along the corridor, landing at Mr. Smithins' feet. "Right, Malone—detention for you!"

"But it wasn't—"

"Double detention!"

Clearly Smithins, who had practically kissed his feet at the hospital the day before, had now changed his tune.

When Eddie dragged himself into detention after school there was only one other pupil there. Ivan Cutler. A scowling Mr. Short—sorry, Mr. Welch—gave them an essay to write about why they shouldn't be cheeky in class, then wandered back outside where he could smoke undisturbed.

The fact that Ivan was blind was no hindrance to his writing an essay. He had a laptop computer and a keypad he was very familiar with. What *was* a hindrance was his complete refusal to do so. He sat behind his desk with his arms folded and a cocky look on his face. "My dad pays for half this school—what're they going to do, expel me if I don't do it? They wouldn't dare."

"Dopey Danvers dared," Eddie pointed out, "she gave you the Bloody Hell."

"Yeah, well, we'll see about that."

Eddie settled down to his essay. Behind him, Ivan lit a cigarette. Eddie glanced up at the smoke alarm in the ceiling. To set off the fire alarm once might be considered unfortunate, but twice would be a catastrophe.

"Please," said Eddie, "just put it out."

"Nope," said Ivan. He puffed merrily away.

Eddie quietly stepped out from his desk, tiptoed back to where Ivan was sitting, and then suddenly ripped the cigarette out of his fingers as he was about to take another drag.

"I'm in enough trouble already, you moron!" Eddie snapped.

"Malone!" Eddie turned. Mr. Short was standing in the doorway. "Smoking in class! Double detention tomorrow as well!"

"Oh bloody great!" Eddie shouted, despite himself.

"Cursing! Triple detention!" yelled Mr. Short.

"What's going on?" Ivan inquired innocently. "I'm only a poor blind boy, can't see what's happening."

"Shut the hell up!" Eddie screamed at him.

"Fourple detention!" Mr. Short screamed, so mad now that he was actually making words up.

Eddie glared at Ivan. Ivan, unaware of it, still sat smirking. Mr. Short ranted and raved about how awful a boy Eddie was and how in his day boys like him would never have been allowed to attend such a prestigious school as Brown's Academy. He was going to make sure Eddie was expelled. He was going to make sure his life was ruined. He was going to make sure . . .

"Hey, dwarf."

Mr. Short—Welch—Short stopped his rant as if he'd been slapped. He looked nervously at Ivan. The smirk had dropped off the blind boy's face; his top lip was slightly curled up into a sneer; even his sunglasses, which before had appeared to be little more than a fashion accessory, seemed to have changed along with his demeanor: the lenses appeared somehow darker, more threatening.

"Mr. Short," Ivan drawled, "I'm *so* tired of you. Please shut up."

"How . . . how . . . d-dare . . . how . . . ," Short stammered.

"I said, shut up. So—shut up. There will be no more detention, for me, or my friend Eddie. Not today, and certainly not tomorrow. Because of you, I've missed my bus, but I was prepared to put up with that because frankly I'm in no hurry to go home. But you—you whiny little midget, you're a much bigger pain in the neck than I imagined. So we're going now. And if you even think of trying to stop us, or reporting us, I'll have my father slice your face to ribbons. Do you understand?"

"Y-yes," said Short, his face now deathly white.

"Good. Now buzz off."

Short's mouth dropped open a fraction—then he abruptly turned on his heel and left the room.

Ivan smiled widely. He clapped his hands together. "Well," he said triumphantly, "that was easy." He stood and held out his arm. "Now, Eddie, get me home and my dad'll give you twenty quid."

Eddie knew that he should say no, that he should go home and forget about Ivan Cutler, Scarface Cutler, the head of Oliver Plunkett. He should reclaim his bunny slippers, watch TV and drink gallons of hot milk. That was the sensible thing to do.

But *sensible* and *Eddie* are two words rarely heard in the same sentence.

Seventeen

It was the biggest house Eddie had ever seen. Well—he had seen bigger houses in movies and on TV, and he had been dragged by his mum and dad around National Trust properties which were way bigger, but for an actual lived-in do-the-dishes tidy-your-room who-tramped-dog's-dirt-into-the-carpet kind of a house, this was certainly the biggest he'd ever seen.

To start with there were huge iron gates set into an enormous white wall which surrounded the property. There were shards of glass set into the cement on top of the wall, and above that several strands of tightly strung barbed wire. In addition security cameras covered every inch of it.

Then there was a long straight driveway leading up to the house itself, which although not particularly tall was exceptionally wide—as if it had started out as a normal house, but then someone had kept adding bits to it whenever they got some spare money. Several low white buildings—outbuildings you'd call them—stood apart from the main house. Some were lying open, and Eddie caught glimpses of cars, some in bits, some looking shiny and new. Others were closed and rather neglected looking. Eddie counted seven of them in all—and each one was bigger than his apartment. There was a pond, a pigeon loft, a tennis court. Over to the left, sitting on the grass, there were three dirt bikes. But Eddie's gaze came back to the outbuildings. One of them was larger than the others; its heavy doors were padlocked shut—and yet there were two men sitting outside it on chairs; just sitting there, doing nothing. They were guards, Eddie was sure of that. But why guard a door when it's securely padlocked?

Because there's something valuable inside. Something like a head.

"Pretty neat place," Eddie said.

"It's all right," said Ivan. "It'll do until we get somewhere bigger."

Eddie wasn't sure if they actually made houses any bigger. "Excellent dirt bikes," he said.

"Oh yeah, they're fun."

"Do you . . . I don't suppose you . . . I suppose your father takes you on them."

"Dad? Nah. He's way too busy. I go on them myself."

"But—"

"I'm blind? Doesn't matter. I have a pretty good idea of the layout of this place. Besides, if I crash the bike, Daddy buys me a new one."

Up ahead of them the large, oak double front doors opened suddenly and a screaming creature charged out.

At least, that was Eddie's first impression: it, she, was wearing a white trouser suit with large pink roses on it; she had masses of mad blond hair tied up above her head like a beehive; her thin legs galloped like a horse to water in a desert. She threw her arms around Ivan and hugged him to her chest. Eddie was surprised she could even lift her arms, she was wearing that much jewelry on them.

"Ivan! Ivan!" she cried. "Ivan! Ivvvvvvvannnnnn!"

Ivan remained impassive. "Yes, Mum."

"Where were you, Ivvvvvvvaannnnnn?"

"School, Mum."

"But you're so late, Ivvvvvvaaannnnnnn, I thought something had happened!"

"Nothing happened, Mum—just missed the bus."

"Oh, sweetie—I was so worried!" She seemed to notice Eddie then for the first time. Her brow furrowed, her eyes narrowed suspiciously. "Who the hell are you?" she snapped.

Eddie's mouth dropped open a fraction, but before he could say anything Ivan said: "This is Eddie. He saved me from the fire yesterday."

A smile swept onto her lips; she let her son go and enveloped Eddie in her gangly, jangly arms. "Oh you darling child!" She kissed his cheek. She kissed his other cheek. And then she kissed him full on the lips, for at least fifteen seconds. Eddie didn't know where to look, or how to get his lips back. Being kissed by a girl was bad enough—or so he imagined—but being kissed by someone's mother, *uuuuuugggggggggggghhhhhhhhhhhh!* And she just wouldn't let go. If she kissed him any harder she'd be able to suck the breakfast out of his stomach. "You saved my baby!" she said finally, letting him go and turning away, hardly aware of Eddie staggering backward and gasping for air. "C'mon inside! I'll make you both a glass of hot milk!"

She hurried away up the steps while Eddie tried to stop himself from being sick.

"C'mon," Ivan said, "I'll give you a tour."

Eddie, clutching his stomach, followed Ivan up the steps, glanced back at the outbuilding one more time, then continued through the front doors and into the palace inside.

For that was what it was. All it lacked was a couple of thrones. There were huge paintings, long luxuriously carpeted corridors, vast rooms, every luxury money could buy, and armed guards to protect it all. Armed guards? There were men, half a dozen of them, sitting at various strategic positions around the house, and they had guns; some of their weapons were visible, sitting on their laps while they read—or pretended to read—their newspapers; other guns were less obvious—a bulge under a jacket, a big lump in a sock. Ivan laughed and joked with these men as he passed, and they laughed and joked back, but Eddie could tell that they were being playful because they were paid to be: he could see it in their eyes, which were cold and deadly.

When they were moving down one of the halls Eddie said: "Why are those guys everywhere? Why do they have guns?"

"Because my father is an important man. He needs to be protected."

"Why?" Eddie asked innocently. "What does he do?"

"I think you know that, Eddie. Everybody knows my dad."

Ivan continued with the tour—there was a cinema room with a huge screen and a vast selection of kids' movies on DVD; there was a games room, with a pool table and half a dozen arcade games; there was a study which had more children's books than most libraries.

"Pretty neat, huh?" said Ivan.

"Yeah. Pretty neat. But do you mind if I ask you something?"

"Fire away."

Eddie glanced nervously back at the armed guard sitting on a chair at the end of the hall. "All these things— the movies, the pool table, the books—I mean, they're fantastic, any kid's dream come true . . . but you're . . . well . . . you're . . ."

"Blind."

"Blind," agreed Eddie.

"I'm blind, so what am I doing with movies and pool and books when I can't see a thing."

"Yeah."

"Well—that's easy, Eddie. You see—I'm not really blind."

"You're . . . you mean you can see?"

"No—I'm blind."

"But you said . . ."

"I know what I said, and I'm not, I'm not really blind. It's just that I can't see."

"What on earth are you talking about?"

Ivan smiled. "It's quite simple. But complicated." Eddie was starting to think that Ivan was barking mad. "When I was five years old I woke up in the middle of the night. I thought I heard voices or I had a nightmare. And like most kids would do, I went to tell my mum or dad. Except I couldn't wake my mum up—she always takes these pills that make her sleep like she's dead. And my dad wasn't there, but I could still hear these voices. So I went downstairs looking for him—and the voices were getting louder, and they weren't just voices—they were screams. Any normal kid would have run back to bed and hid under the blankets, but not me. I followed the sounds, down through the kitchen, out the back door and across to one of the outbuildings. There was a light on, there were people inside. I sneaked up to a window and looked in."

He stopped there for a moment, and took a deep breath. He took his sunglasses off and rubbed at his eyes. It was the first time Eddie had seen him without his sunglasses; somehow it made him look smaller, weaker, more vulnerable. He quickly slipped them back on.

"What . . . what did you see?"

"There was a man . . . tied to a chair . . . he was all sweaty and there was such . . . fear in his eyes . . . he was looking up at this other man like he was the devil himself. This other man, he stepped forward and I could see he had a knife in his hand and I thought he was just going to threaten him or something . . . but instead he slashed at his face . . . and there was blood everywhere and the man in the chair was screaming . . . and then the man with the knife turned to speak to one of the other men and I saw his face for the first time . . . and it was my dad . . . and he was laughing . . . and I was so shocked I stumbled back from the window and I must have tripped over something and I fell over and banged my head and got knocked out. That's where they found me in the morning. They took me to the hospital and I was unconscious for three days, and when I finally did wake up I couldn't see. Couldn't see anything. Blind as a bat. Although bats have radar."

Ivan shrugged sadly.

Eddie was confused—he felt sympathetic, of course, the story was a horrific one, but Ivan had also just claimed that he could see after all. "I don't under—"

"It's quite simple, Eddie. There's nothing actually wrong with my eyes. I've had all the tests. They're in perfect working order. I just can't see a thing."

"I still—"

"They say it's a psychological thing. Obviously my dad told them I'd had a nightmare—he wasn't about to admit to cutting somebody's face up—but they knew exactly who he was, they weren't fooled for one moment. They think I was so shocked by what I saw that my brain tried to block it out by closing down my sight. Like it was an electric switch that just got turned to the 'off' position. But then I fell and banged my head and the switch got stuck in the 'off' position."

"God," said Eddie.

"Yeah—well, he's no help either, though my mum spends half of every day praying to him. Look around the house, Eddie, there's little crosses and religious statues everywhere. They say my sight will come back someday, Eddie—they just can't say when. Maybe it'll take another bang on the head. Maybe the 'off' button will just work itself loose and switch back on. But to answer your original question—why I have all these DVDs and computer games and books? My mum and dad are totally convinced that my sight is going to come back and that's why they buy all this stuff for me, so it's ready and waiting when I can finally see again."

"Oh," said Eddie. "Well, that's nice."

"No it's not," snapped Ivan, "it's *sick*, that's what it is. I'm blind and they just won't face up to it. I'm blind and my dad made me blind, that's the truth of it. I'm blind and my mum keeps thinking up these mad schemes to make me see again and they never work. I'm blind and my dad's the worst gangster in the country and he makes all this money and spends it all on things I can't use or play with because I'm blind, because he blames himself for what happened. I hate my mum and I hate my dad and I just want to be able to see again."

His cheeks were flushed with anger.

Eddie shrugged helplessly, then realized that Ivan couldn't actually see the shrug. "Sorry," he said.

"Not your fault," said Ivan.

At the very end of the hall Ivan's mum appeared with two steaming mugs in her hand.

"Ivaaaaaan! Eddddddddie! I have your hot milk!"

Ivan turned and yelled: "Why don't you pour it down your knickers, you old cow!"

Eddie didn't know where to look.

"Oh, *Ivaaaaan!*" his mum shouted back. "You are *so* cheeky!"

"I'm not being cheeky, I'm serious, you rat-faced old horse!" Ivan's mum laughed and turned back into the kitchen. "Come and get it!" she shouted back.

Ivan shook his head and smiled at Eddie. "See, they feel so bad about what happened, they let me get away with murder." And then his face hardened a little as he added: "Just like my dad."

Ivan turned and walked toward the kitchen.

Eddie swallowed, then followed.

As he walked a familiar phrase crept into his mind, and it didn't make him feel any more comfortable. Scarface Cutler was a murderer. But what if it really was a case of like father, like son?

Eighteen

Eddie came through the door at about six o'clock. Before he had a chance to take off his purple blazer his mum shouted from the kitchen. "Oh—there you are at last!"

"Sorry, Mum, I missed the train. . . ."

"Come on through, Eddie—your little friends are here!"

Eddie's brow furrowed. He didn't really have any friends, little or large. He stepped into the kitchen, and blinked in disbelief at the sight of Mo and Pat sitting at his kitchen table about to tuck into burgers and chips. They smiled nervously at him.

"Hi . . . ," he began, then looked at his mum, who was just setting down a plate at the chair where he usually sat. "I don't . . ."

"Well . . . they called for you and I was going to chase them . . . and I thought . . . well, I've never really given them a chance, have I? You've a right to choose your own friends, don't you? Just like I've the right to choose Mr. Scuttles, isn't that right?"

Eddie nodded vaguely.

She patted his seat. "So come on, sit yourself down. A special tea for a special boy. My hero!"

Eddie sat. Mo grinned at him. "Nice blazer," she said.

"At least I have one," he snapped back.

Mo made a face.

"Pat's been telling me all about your little gang," said his mum. "It must be such fun! You're just like the Famous Five! Except . . . there's only three of you. But still, what adventures you can have! Oh to be your age again."

Eddie's mum smiled contentedly off into the distance. Eddie picked up his burger and bit into it. He looked daggers at Pat. And then at Mo. Behind them something was pushed through the letter box.

"That'll be the paper!" said Eddie's mum, and she jumped up to get it.

Eddie took advantage of her momentary absence to whisper across the table: "What are you doing here? What are you doing telling her about the gang? Are you mental or something?"

"We were worried about you!" Mo whispered back. "We were supposed to meet you off the train, you never showed up."

Eddie shook his head. "I got put in detention. Then I had to go back to Ivan Cutler's house."

"You went to his house?" Pat asked. "Did you see—"

"No, I didn't see the head." Pat immediately looked disappointed. "What do you think they're going to do, have it sitting on a coffee table? Or hanging over the fireplace?"

Pat shrugged. "No, I just—"

"But I've a good idea where it is."

"You—?" Pat's eyes danced with excitement, but before Eddie could say anything else Mo shushed them as Eddie's mum came back in and sat at the table. She unfolded a copy of the *Belfast Telegraph* and held it up as she opened it to the entertainment section inside.

"You know," she was saying, her face now hidden from view, "I haven't been to the cinema in so long, I thought Bernard and I could maybe go and see a movie tonight— you don't mind that, do you, Eddie?"

She peered out from behind the paper. So that was why she was being so nice—she wanted to go out with Scuttles. Eddie hated Scuttles with a passion, but just for once he was going to go along with it; he needed to talk through his plans with Mo and Pat.

"No, that's fine, Mum, you go out and enjoy yourself."

"That's a good boy." She smiled and disappeared back behind the paper. "Now it's just a question of what. Let me see . . . something nice and romantic, I think. Who's this Jackie Chan fella?"

Eddie smirked across at Mo, but she was suddenly looking very panicked indeed; she was pointing urgently at the front of the paper. Eddie followed her gaze. The main headline across the top read: HUNT INTENSIFIES FOR HEAD OF OLIVER PLUNKETT. Beneath that there was a photo of the Primate of All Ireland and then a smaller headline that read: PRIMATE REFUSES TO

PAY RANSOM. But it was a third, even smaller headline and photograph that was causing Mo such distress. It was a photo of Pat. It appeared to be a year or two out of date, but it was definitely Pat. RUNAWAY ORPHAN MAY BE SEARCHING FOR SAINT'S HEAD, said the headline.

Mo made a *what'll we do?* gesture with her hands.

Eddie's mum said, "Or maybe we'll just go for a nice meal . . . HOLY GOD!"

She shot suddenly back in her chair, dropping the newspaper. There had been a flash of something past Eddie's eyes, and it took several moments for him to realize what it was: a hamburger traveling at about a hundred miles an hour.

His mum jumped to her feet. "What *on earth* are you doing?" she shouted across the table at Pat, who was the only one of them now minus a hamburger.

"Sorry," Pat said rather sheepishly, "it just . . . slipped out of my hands."

"Slipped?" Eddie's mum looked incredulous. She pressed her hand to her chest. "You nearly gave me a heart attack."

"I . . . dropped it," said Pat, "and trying to catch it, I just . . . somehow hit it instead and it . . . flew across the table."

It was the stupidest, lamest excuse, but Eddie's mum appeared to accept it. "Well, just be careful." She raised the paper and examined where the burger had struck it: Pat's aim had been perfect. He'd not only hit his own photograph dead center, he'd also successfully smeared ketchup right across it. They held their breath as Eddie's mum picked up a napkin and wiped it across the stain.

She balled up the napkin and set it back on the table, then raised the paper again; they let their breath out when they saw that although she'd wiped the ketchup off, it had soaked into the paper, smudging Pat's face so that he was no longer recognizable.

A few moments later Eddie's mum set the newspaper down. "I'll just give Bernard a wee call," she said, and left the table. "Eddie, can I have a word?"

Eddie winked at Pat and Mo as he followed his mum into the lounge. She closed the door after him, then waved an angry finger in his face. "Eddie—I was prepared to give your friends a chance, but I want them out of the house now."

"But why?"

"*Why?* Because that little terror tried to murder me with a hamburger."

"Mum—he didn't, it slipped, he—"

"He threw it at me as hard as he could!"

"He didn't, Mum, why would—"

"I don't know why! Because he's trouble! Eddie, for goodness' sake, you're a good boy, but you're far too trusting. Have you ever *accidentally* thrown a hamburger at someone? Of course you haven't. My God, if it had been a quarter pounder he'd have taken my head off. And how would that have looked on my gravestone. *Mrs. Malone— Killed by Flying Hamburger—Rest in Peace.*"

She managed a smile. She ruffled his hair. "I just worry about you, son."

"I'm fine. And so are they."

She sighed. "Well, just not tonight, eh? I'm going out

with Bernard, I don't want them hanging around here when I'm out, okay? And I'm sure you've got homework to do."

She went off then to phone Scuttles and get ready, and Eddie walked his friends to the door.

Mo blew air out of her cheeks. "That was close," she said.

"It was all I could think of," said Pat.

"It's okay," said Eddie, "just don't make it a habit. Okay. Give me about an hour until she goes out, then I'll see you downstairs and we'll go over our plans."

He began to close the door.

But Pat couldn't contain himself. "What about the head? Are you sure it's there? Is everything okay for the party? Do you think you can get at it? Is there—"

"Shhhhhh . . . ," Eddie said, holding up a finger and glancing behind him to make sure his mother hadn't reappeared. "Everything's organized. I spoke to Ivan's mum. She said there'll be dozens of kids at the party anyway, so the more the merrier. So all four of us are going to the party."

Pat clapped his hands together. "Excellent!"

But Mo was frowning. "All four of us?" she said. Eddie nodded. "You, me, Pat and *who*, exactly?" She gave him a hard look. "You're not bringing your mum, Eddie."

Eddie laughed. "No, of course not."

"Well, who then?"

He counted around them. "You, me, Pat, oh yeah . . . and the explosives expert."

"The—" Mo and Pat began together, but he closed the door on them before they could say another word.

Nineteen

The day of Ivan Cutler's birthday party was hot and sticky, a September day that would have sat more comfortably with its steamy friends, July or early August. It seemed longer than other days: the clocks, in identical positions on identical walls in identical classrooms throughout Brown's Academy, seemed to slow down; the teachers moved and talked as if they were wading through custard, speaking through jelly. Eddie tried to concentrate on geography and math and on not getting detention, but all he could think about was the head and how they were going to steal it, about how they were going to negotiate its return to the church, about what heroes they'd be and how much of a reward they'd be given.

That was, if it all went according to plan.

But when, in his short life, had anything gone according to plan?

Well, it had to start sometime. No better day than today. He was older now. He was maturing into a fine gang leader. Hadn't he outsmarted Bacon and Bap and the rest of the Reservoir Pups? Hadn't he befriended Ivan Cutler and managed to get four invites to his party? Hadn't he pinpointed the exact position of Oliver Plunkett's head and devised a scheme for rescuing it?

Oh yes, the scheme.

It depended, quite a lot, on an explosion.

For which was required: one explosives expert.

Even in a place like Belfast, explosives experts don't exactly grow on trees. He therefore considered it a very good omen that there happened to be a bomb expert in this very school.

Well, not exactly a bomb expert. But certainly someone who knew how to blow things up. Albeit, usually by accident.

Gary Gilmore wasn't easy to recruit. Eddie approached him at lunchtime and asked him if he wanted to go to a birthday party.

"No," said Gary.

"Ivan Cutler's party, there'll be stacks of things to do. He has dirt bikes, arcade games, a pool table, there's even going to be fireworks later on."

"No. I hate Ivan Cutler."

"He likes you, wants you to come."

"I wouldn't go if it was the last party on earth."

Eddie sighed, slipped his arm around Gary's shoulders and said: "Can I let you into a secret?"

"No," said Gary. "I don't want to know, secrets get me into trouble. I'm in enough trouble. The police called at my house last night. They wanted to know if I'd set fire to the school. Of course I denied it. I blamed you."

Eddie took his arm away. "You blamed me?"

"No, of course I didn't. But that's what I mean. Secrets. I don't like them."

"Okay—okay. Then let me tell you the truth. About why I want you to come to Ivan Cutler's party."

Gary shrugged.

"I am the leader of one of the most dangerous gangs in the city, I . . . what are you laughing at?"

"You?"

"Yes, me."

"I can't imagine you as the leader of anything."

"Well, I am, okay?"

"What's your name?"

"Eddie."

"No, the gang's name."

"We don't have a name, that's how big a secret we are."

"I don't like secrets."

"Will you just listen?" Eddie was ready to throttle him. But he needed him. He had to keep his temper, keep calm. Gary finally realized how serious Eddie was; the cheeky smile which had sat on his face from the start of their conversation slipped away. "Okay," said Eddie, "I run this gang, and we're trying to get back the head of

Oliver Plunkett. You do know about the head of Oliver Plunkett?"

"Yes, of course, who doesn't?"

"It's at Ivan's house."

"Ivan's?"

"Yes, Ivan's."

"You mean Scarface Cutler's?"

"Yes, Scarface Cutler's."

"Scarface I'll-cut-your-face-to-ribbons Cutler's house?"

"Yes, I think we've established that."

"Scarface I-really-do-have-the-most-dangerous-gang-in-the-city Cutler's house?"

"*Yes*, Gary."

"You want to steal Oliver Plunkett's head from Scarface Cutler?"

"Yes."

"You want to steal Oliver Plunkett's head from under the nose of the Scarface Cutler gang, the most blood-thirsty outfit in the history of bloodthirsty outfits?"

"Yes, Gary."

"You're bloody mad."

"That may be, but we need your help."

"They'd kill us all. But torture us first."

"Only if we're caught. We want you to join us."

"No way."

"We have to get the head back."

"No way."

"If we don't the primate will be embarrassed and he won't become pope."

"Doesn't worry me."

"The head's worth three million euros, we'll probably get a cut of that."

"No good to you if you're dead."

"We need you, Gary."

"No, no, no, no, no, no."

"You get to blow things up."

"Well, why didn't you say?" The cheeky grin was suddenly back on Gary's face.

Eddie smiled back. "Well," he said, putting his arm back around Gary, "this is the plan. . . ."

Eddie was surprised to find that almost everyone else in the class was going to the party as well.

"But don't you all hate him?" he said to one group of boys at lunchtime.

"So? He's got a great house, and great computer games."

"And the fireworks are great. We go every year."

"But . . . but . . . you never talk to him at school, you treat him like he's got a disease or something."

"He has got a disease."

"Blindness isn't a disease."

"Don't mean that. He's got a disease of the head. It makes him miserable and a bully and a liar and a squealer. We don't like Ivan Cutler, but we can put up with him for one day."

Another boy said: "We feel sorry for him, having a dad like Scarface, but it's no excuse for being such a miserable big wart."

"Well, why don't you try and be more friendly toward him then?"

"Tried that," said another boy, "and he punched me in the willy and stole my pencil case. Then I got detention for trying to hit the blind boy."

"And I tried to help him across the road, and he pushed me in front of a car, nearly killed me."

"And I offered to share my homework with him and he stole it, then told the teacher I was copying him. I nearly got suspended."

"He's bad through and through."

"He's evil."

"He's a spoilt bully and he deserves a good kicking."

"Great parties, though."

"Fantastic."

Eddie looked incredulously at them. "Don't you think he knows that you're just using him?"

The boys weren't taken aback by this at all. "Course he does. But what choice has he got? He hasn't got any other friends. Apart from you. So his dad comes to the rescue like he always does—he buys his only son some friends for his birthday."

Eddie sighed. "That's quite sad, really."

"Yeah," said one of the boys, "but great fireworks."

And it was the fireworks that would be the key to it all.

Twenty

It wasn't a day to get tangled up with Bacon or Bap, so Eddie arranged to meet Mo and Pat off the train one stop before Botanic Station. From there they walked to Ivan Cutler's house. They didn't say much on the way: they were nervous about what was to come, and also Eddie was annoyed with Pat who, for the second night in a row, had fallen asleep in his bed before Eddie had a chance to get into it. Eddie had spent the night on the floor, feverishly dreaming about the day ahead—that was, when he got any sleep at all, as Pat had had another nightmare about the head of Oliver Plunkett.

But now it was D-Day. O-Day. P-Day. Whatever you wanted to call it.

"Be careful, stick to the plan, and we'll be fine," Eddie said as they approached the gates, which were decorated with green and white streamers. "And remember, Scarface Cutler is possibly the most vicious criminal this city has ever seen."

"Thanks for that," said Mo.

Mrs. Cutler opened the gate herself and ushered them in. She was wearing white again, and although it didn't seem possible, even more jewelry. She rattled her arms at them as she directed them into the house, past the bouncy castle, past the dirt bikes, past the trestle tables straining under mountains of food, past the armed guards who were doing their best to smile and look happy while still appearing alert and dangerous.

There were already around twenty boys present, and maybe six girls, but as every minute passed more and more arrived until the house and garden were packed with screaming and laughing kids charging about, bouncing on the castle, arguing over the dirt bikes, yelling for a go on the arcade games, tearing great holes in the pool table, throwing water bombs, spilling crisps, dancing to music, playing football, and generally having a great time—except wherever Ivan appeared. When he entered the pool room, boys set down the cues and went off to play outside. When he went outside, boys stopped their football game and hurried indoors. Where he went he seemed to suck the joy and happiness out of his surroundings, which was a pity, because it was his birthday, his party. Eddie felt a little bit sorry for him. He gave him a present—a book Eddie had already read. But he made sure the Jaffa cake crumbs were poured out of it and the sneeze stains on page 184 were dry before he wrapped it. It didn't matter in the end. Ivan just tossed it unopened into a pile with the others.

"Aren't you going to open it?" Eddie asked.

"It's a book. I'm blind."

"You said your sight would come back."

"*No*, my parents said it would come back."

"Oh. Well. Sorry. Perhaps I could read it to you."

"Perhaps you could just get me something better?"

Eddie sighed. This wasn't going very well. At this rate he'd be thrown out before he had a chance to steal the head. "So," he said, sounding vaguely desperate, "great party."

"Yeah, *right*," said Ivan.

"No, really, everyone's saying—" but before he could finish lying, a large hand was brought down suddenly on his shoulders. He looked up into the intense, icy blue eyes of Scarface Cutler. "How're you doing, kid?" the gangster boomed. "Enjoying the party?"

"Yeah, magic," said Eddie.

"He brought me a book," said Ivan.

"Excellent!" said Scarface. "That's the spirit!" He clapped Eddie on the shoulders again. "You're the guest of honor, Eddie—saved my boy from the fire! Come on and get a hot dog!"

He began to lead Eddie away. Eddie looked back at Ivan and shrugged helplessly. But, of course, Ivan couldn't see.

Scarface led Eddie out of the house and down the steps toward where one of his guards was sitting behind a barbecue cooking the hot dogs. The guard didn't look too happy about it.

"Hot dog, my man, for my man!"

The guard shoveled a hot dog into a roll and disconsolately handed it across to Eddie.

"Ah, it's great to be young," Scarface said as he looked around his expansive garden at all the kids having fun. "And it's great to have friends. Eddie, I know all these kids aren't really Ivan's friends. I know he can be difficult. That's my fault, really. Can't be easy, having a dad like me." Eddie didn't know whether to nod or shrug. So he took a bite of his hot dog and made a kind of grunting noise. "I live in a dangerous world, Eddie, and I'm not always going to be here. So I worry about what'll happen to my son when I'm gone. I need to know there'll be someone here to look after him. I don't mean his mum, of course she'll do her best. I mean a friend, someone who'll keep him out of trouble, or, if he gets into it, get him out of it. Do you understand what I'm saying, Eddie?" Eddie grunted again. "Will you do that for him, Eddie, will you promise me that you'll look after him?"

Not in a million years.

He thought it, but he couldn't possibly say it. He gave a third grunt, and moved his head about a bit, somewhere between a nod and a shake.

"Then put it here," said Scarface, and extended his hand.

Eddie had two choices: shake his hand or run away.

Naturally, given that Scarface Cutler was a cold-blooded killer, he shook his hand.

It's not worth the paper it's not written on; that's what he told himself; but it seemed to satisfy Scarface. He winked at Eddie. "That's my boy!" he said. "Now—enjoy the rest of the party!"

● ● ●

Eddie, Mo and Pat made a point of not hanging around together. They didn't want to look too much like a gang. But from time to time during the course of the afternoon they managed to compare notes.

"I checked the outbuilding," Pat said. "I see what you mean about the padlock. It's huge."

"The guard sneaks off every half hour to get a hot dog," said Mo. "We could—"

"No," said Eddie, "it's too risky. We have to wait for nightfall. We have to wait for the fireworks."

Mo nodded.

They met up again close to eight o'clock. The sky was already beginning to darken.

"He's not here, is he?" said Mo. "The explosives guy."

"He will be."

Eddie was sure the fireworks wouldn't start until it was pitch black. Still, Gary Gilmore was definitely late. There was no getting away from it. He looked around the grounds, at the litter, at the food carelessly thrown away, at the sweaty faces of the boys and girls still running around, but they weren't quite as fast, not quite as enthusiastic. With fatigue there would come arguments, tears, upset. What if the decision was made to start the fireworks early?

Where was Gilmore?

They agreed to meet behind the house in twenty minutes. It would be dark by then and if Gilmore hadn't arrived they would either have to abandon their plan or come up with something else, and quick. Eddie looked at Pat: his face was set hard and serious; he was here for the head, no doubt about it, and he wouldn't be put off.

Eddie wandered back into the house to use the toilet. There were two downstairs—one was already occupied, the other was blocked with toilet roll and was overflowing onto the tiles. So he went upstairs in search of another. He tried four different doors but found only bedrooms. Finally he discovered that the fifth door led into a huge pink-tiled bathroom with a tub capable of bathing an entire family all at once, plus their pet elephant. As Eddie had a pee he noticed a second door to his left, presumably leading to another bedroom. He could hear muffled sounds coming from behind it. The sensible thing would just have been to finish and flush and go back to the party, but as we have noted before, *sensible* and *Eddie* are two words rarely heard in the same sentence. To this we can add another old phrase: curiosity killed the cat.

Quite simply, Eddie couldn't resist.

He was a brave gang leader, and, as Captain Black had once told him, to paraphrase, knowledge is power.

Also, he was dead nosey.

Eddie opened the door a fraction; he looked and listened.

At first he was a little confused, because the sound didn't match the pictures. He could see Ivan's mum, lying on top of a large bed, drinking from a large glass of what appeared to be red wine. But he could *hear* a storm raging, he could hear lightning and rain and people shouting over the roar of it. And then it stopped suddenly. Then after a few seconds it started again—the same sounds, the same shouts. Eddie saw Mrs. Cutler raise something and point it across the room, out of his field of vision. He took the chance of opening the door a fraction wider . . . ah, he could see now, a large television, she was pointing a remote control at it.

What was she doing in here, watching TV with her son's birthday party in full swing downstairs?

Eddie was drawn back to the pictures on the TV—hey, he recognized this. Ivan's mum was watching a movie, an old black-and-white one Eddie had watched with his dad once on late-night TV—*Frankenstein*. It was at the scene where the mad scientist had built the creature out of dead body parts and was about to bring it to life by harnessing the power of lightning and feeding it into the mismatched body of the monster he had created. Ivan's mum was watching that scene, then rewinding it and watching it again, and again, and again. Maybe she was drunk. It was a good scene, but it wasn't *that* good.

Then the main bedroom door opened, and Scarface entered the room. Eddie quickly closed the bathroom door; but he couldn't bring himself to leave; he was too busy listening to Ivan's parents argue with one another.

"What are you doing watching that rubbish again?" Scarface roared.

"It's not rubbish, it's science!"

"It's garbage! Now come down, we're going to cut the cake!"

"No, I'm watching, please . . . it can work."

Eddie heard Scarface cross the room. "Please, give me the controls."

"No, it can work . . . it can work. . . ."

"Don't be daft, now give me the controls, come on. I'll pay for whatever operation he needs, but not this, not this."

"No! Operations don't work! We've tried that! This is the only way!"

Then Scarface must have grabbed the remote control, for something smashed against the door Eddie was listening behind. He jumped back, then darted back out into the hall. He raced down it, then took the stairs three at a time. By the time Scarface appeared at the top of the stairs Eddie was watching some of the other boys trying to play on the ripped pool table.

"All right, everyone!" Scarface cried, clapping his hands together. "It's time for the fireworks!"

Twenty-one

Everyone converged on the front lawn, including, Eddie was pleased to see, all of the guards. Not just the ones who'd helped out with the food and organized the dirt bikes, but also the two who'd sat outside the outbuilding where they hoped to find the head of Oliver Plunkett. Setting off fireworks was not a one-man business, at least not the kind of show Scarface intended to put on for his son. Nothing but the best—there were hundreds and hundreds of fireworks lined up on the grass, and they all had to be lit individually—which meant at least half a dozen pairs of adult hands.

Mo found Eddie. "Where's Pat?" were Eddie's first words.

"Watching the outbuilding. He's itching to get started. Any sign of whatsisname, Gilmore?"

Eddie was already shaking his head when he caught

sight of his explosives expert hurrying up the driveway. He was just about to wave him over when a guard he hadn't seen before suddenly stepped out from the cover of some bushes and stopped him.

"No!" said Eddie, a little too loudly. Then he realized that the guard was only directing Gary away from the line of fire of the fireworks. Gary skirted round the side of the launch site and came toward them.

"Where were you?" Eddie demanded.

"Sorry," said Gary, trying to catch his breath, "I had to run all the way. The police called again. They questioned me forever and ever about the fire in the science block. The good news is, I think I convinced them it wasn't me."

"Good," said Eddie, "now—"

"Bad news is they now think it was you. I swear to God I didn't tell them anything."

"There's nothing to tell!"

"I know! But they think there is! They're on their way to your house."

Eddie sighed. "Great. And I suppose with police swarming all over your house, you weren't able to do your . . . *thing.* . . ."

Gary smiled. "Are you joking? Of course I was." He produced what looked like a small lump of modeling clay with a small piece of plastic attached to it from his pocket. "Those guys wouldn't know a bomb from an ashtray. This, my friends—and I don't know you," he said, nodding at Mo, "but I guess you're a friend—this is my new invention. The microbomb."

"It looks," Mo said, seemingly reading Eddie's thought, "like modeling clay with a bit of plastic stuck to it."

Gary nodded. "It's supposed to. Whereas in fact it's a plastic explosive with a microchip attached."

Mo looked at it more closely. "Why a microchip?"

"Good question," said Gary. He pulled around a small canvas bag that had been hanging unnoticed over his shoulder and patted it. "I have a miniature laptop computer in here. I key in the exact dimensions, weight and density of the item you need destroyed, I scan a picture of it—and then when I send the signal to set off the bomb, it destroys only what it's instructed to, causes the minimum of damage to the surrounding building and very little noise. It's what I call a VSB, a Very Smart Bomb."

"Impressive," said Eddie.

"Do we have time to do all that?" Mo asked.

Gary rolled his eyes. "It only takes a fraction of a second. It's built for speed."

Behind them the crowd standing waiting for the fireworks began to count down from ten. Then one by one, and then two by two and on into larger groups, the fireworks shot up into the night sky and exploded. Eddie could see Ivan Cutler standing at the front of the crowd. He didn't look happy. His mother stood behind him, her hands on his shoulders as if she was keeping him in place. He seemed to jump a little each time a firework went off; his father, on the other hand, was running up and down cheering and clapping his hands and encouraging his guards to work faster. He was enjoying the birthday party much more than his son, almost as if it was his own party. Maybe when you were a mad nuthouse killer like Scarface Cutler you didn't get to have birthday parties, because nobody would come.

Mo tugged at Eddie's arm. "C'mon," she said.

They hurried around the side of the house, and joined Pat close to the back door. The grass swept away in front of them to the series of outbuildings.

"Well?" Eddie whispered.

"All clear," said Pat.

They waited for a lull in the fireworks. As soon as the sky darkened Eddie whispered, "Let's go," then the four of them padded softly across the close-cut lawn to the outbuilding they were after. As they crowded in around the door Gary removed a small torch from his canvas bag and hurriedly examined the heavy padlock: then he took out his laptop and typed in its measurements. When he'd finished he examined the figures, made some adjustments, then affixed the small ball of plastic explosives to the padlock.

"Okay," he said, "let's just move around the corner here, and I'll set this little baby off."

They stood under the protection of the whitewashed side wall of the outbuilding, their hearts thumping, their breathing labored. As Gary reached for the detonator button Eddie suddenly said, "Wait. Wait for the next big flurry of fireworks."

Gary nodded. Several small fireworks arced up into the night sky; they hissed and rotated, but provided little noise. Three more sprayed down like a waterfall. But then they saw a dozen pinpoints of light shoot into the air. . . .

"Ready . . . ," said Eddie.

The pinpoints exploded together, creating the greatest racket yet.

"Now!" yelled Eddie.

Gary pushed the button.

And their whole world shook.

Eddie, Gary, Mo and Pat were thrown to the ground while bricks and shards of wood rained down around them.

It was several moments before Eddie realized that he was not in fact dead, and even longer before his hearing came back. He struggled back to his feet. He gave Mo a helping hand. Pat rose beside him. Gary remained on the ground, surveying the destruction and shaking his head.

"I think I might have put the decimal point in the wrong place," he said weakly.

"Might?" said Mo, still coughing her way out of a cloud of smoke and dust.

Eddie couldn't believe that so little explosive could cause so much damage. The walls had buckled and broken; the roof had caved in; the door had blown off its hinges and lay in a dozen pieces halfway across the garden.

Terrified now, they all looked toward the corner of the house, certain that Scarface Cutler and his gang were about to charge around it.

But the fireworks continued to whoosh and bang across the sky.

Eddie raced to the corner of the house and peered around. The show was continuing all right.

No one had noticed. Or if they had, they'd thought it was all part of the display.

They had caused what was without doubt a major

explosion—but by some miracle they had gotten away with it.

Eddie hurried back. Pat was already tearing away at the rubble."It's here, it must be here. You better not have destroyed it, you better not. . . ."

The others quickly joined him, throwing bricks away behind them as if their lives depended on it.

"It's a wooden box," Pat was saying urgently, "it's dark wood, it has silver bits engraved on it."

"Like this?" said Mo.

Mo was holding a dusty but intact ornate wooden box.

"Bingo!" shouted Pat. He ran forward and tried to wrestle it from Mo's grasp, but Mo pulled it away from him. "Not now!" she snapped, and darted a look at Eddie.

Eddie nodded. "Pat, we have to get out of here, fast. Leave it until later!"

Pat nodded reluctantly. Mo borrowed Gary's canvas bag and squeezed the wooden box inside it.

Now for the escape.

Eddie had briefly considered trying to get over the wall. It was close, but there was barbed wire, and it was guarded by security cameras. No. He had decided that they would rejoin the crowd and hope to slip out unnoticed as the party ended. It wouldn't be long—the last of the fireworks were just dropping out of the sky as the four of them sauntered back into the front garden. They stuck close together, keeping as much of the canvas bag hidden as they could. Up ahead, at the end of the driveway, parents were already arriving to pick up their kids.

As the final act of the party, Ivan's mum emerged from

the house and led the party guests in a rather halfhearted rendition of "Happy Birthday." She thanked everyone for coming and signaled to two of the security guards to open the front gates. As the children began to stream away some of them mumbled birthday good wishes to Ivan; but most of them ignored him. Eddie thought he cut rather a tragic figure as he walked past him, and he thought briefly of Scarface's plea to him to look after his son if anything happened to him; but what was he supposed to do, adopt him?

As they approached the front gate, Eddie saw that the two security guards who'd opened the gates had been joined by two others. Perhaps they just wanted to make sure everyone was successfully reunited with their parents. Perhaps they were concerned about guests stealing toys from the house. Either way, it made for a nerve-wracking few moments. Eddie did his best to smile and chat with Mo; Mo stared ahead and nodded; Gary's face was a mask of sweat; Pat was biting down hard on his lip.

They were just passing the guards when a harsh voice shouted: "HEY!"

Scarface Cutler.

They froze.

Other boys made space around them as Scarface Cutler hurried up.

Under his breath Pat muttered, "Run, run, run, run."

But the security guards were right beside them, there was no way they could escape.

"EDDIE!"

Mo looked at Eddie in desperation, *make a decision, Eddie, make a decision, lead us, lead us . . .*

It was too late. Scarface clamped his huge hands down on Eddie's shoulders and then turned him so that he could look into his eyes.

"I think you've forgotten something, Eddie," he said.

Eddie could only think of the knife that would soon go *slice, slice, slice.*

"I . . . I . . . ," Eddie began.

And then Scarface surprised him completely by smiling and holding up a small green paper bag.

"I think you forgot your goody bag, Eddie."

Eddie's mouth dropped open a fraction. Out of the corner of his eye he was dimly aware that the other kids were all holding identical bags. They must have been distributed during the firework display.

Scarface thrust a bag into Eddie's hands. "I put an extra tenner in it," he said, "for being a good friend." Then he winked, ruffled Eddie's hair and strode away back up the drive.

Eddie's legs had no strength in them at all now. Mo, Pat and Gary, themselves grinning stupidly with the relief of their reprieve, more or less carried him through the gates. They pushed through the lines of waiting parents, and then guided him down the road away from the Cutler mansion.

Only when they were round the corner and out of sight did they stop and look at each other.

We've done it!

We've stolen back the head of Oliver Plunkett!

They danced and yelled and hugged each other.

We've done it!

Twenty-two

These were, of course, FAMOUS LAST WORDS.

When they had finished congratulating each other on how wonderful they were, they immediately started arguing.

"C'mon," Pat said, "we have to get to the train station, get back to Drogheda."

Mo looked at her watch. "It's after ten, Pat, the last train will already have—"

"Then we get a taxi! The primate will pay for it, we can—"

"No," Eddie said firmly, "we have to discuss it."

"Discuss *what*?" Pat cried. "There's nothing to discuss!"

"Yes there is, Pat, we can't just hand the head back, there'll have to be . . . negotiations."

"Negotiate what? What are you talking about? We have to save the primate."

"Yes, I understand that . . . but . . ." Eddie was not entirely sure where he was going, he was just sure that it all wouldn't be as straightforward as Pat seemed to think.

"Well," he began again, "we've expended a lot of energy and effort getting the head back. We should negotiate some sort of compensation for our—"

"You want to be *paid* for saving the head of Oliver Plunkett?" Pat asked incredulously.

Eddie blinked at Mo. "We are a gang, we do have expenses. . . ."

Mo shook her head sadly. "Eddie, that's not why we did this. . . ."

"I know, I know that," said Eddie. "All the same, the head's worth three million euros . . . think what we could do with a fraction of that." He was supposed to be this tremendous and terrifying gang leader, yet he was becoming painfully aware that he couldn't argue his way out of a paper bag. He cast a despairing look at Gary for support.

"Don't look at me," Gary said, "I just want to blow things up."

Eddie cleared his throat. "Don't get me wrong, guys, I want the head returned as much as you do. But we have to be certain it's going into the right hands. We can't just send Pat off in a taxi, we might never see him again."

"So it's not the money you want," said Pat, his words heavy with sarcasm, "it's just you have concerns for the head."

"Y-yes, of c-course," Eddie stammered. "We need to work out a strategy for getting it back, and there's going to be a lot of interest in this. Mo, you know what it's like, there'll be TV and radio—there'll be book people and film companies and—"

"Haven't you forgotten someone?" a man's voice boomed out of the darkness.

They spun around—and were immediately blinded as full-beam car headlights were switched on.

Eddie felt his stomach drop into his feet.

Instead of making their getaway, they had stood arguing amongst themselves only a few hundred meters from the Cutler house. Scarface had surely discovered the destroyed outbuilding and sent his guards out to find the culprits. Now they would all be tortured and killed.

The figure of a man moved through the beams of light toward them. Pat, who'd been holding the bag containing Plunkett's head, took a step back, and the others moved instinctively to protect him. All except Gary, who ran off into the darkness. *What a coward*, Eddie thought.

Then the man was right up close and gazing greedily down at them. "Movies, books, television, radio . . . what about newspapers?"

"Crumples," Pat muttered. The journalist from the *Belfast Telegraph*.

"You got it!" Crumples cried as his eyes fell on the bag and the tip of the wooden box peeking out of it.

Pat held the box even closer to his chest. "So what?" he snapped. "It's mine."

"I thought we had an agreement, young fella," said Crumples, "*and* I paid you more than a hundred and fifty euros."

"You can have the money back," said Pat, backing away, "just leave us alone."

"Yeah, disappear," said Eddie, not feeling half as brave as he sounded.

"We got it," said Mo, "it's got nothing to do with you."

A cruel smile appeared on Crumples' face—then his left hand shot out and slapped Eddie hard across the side of his head. Eddie reeled away. His ear felt like it was on fire. Crumples quickly struck out at Mo and Pat as well, but they both managed to skip out of the way. Pat started to run, but Crumples kicked out and just managed to trip him. Pat fell heavily, but still held firmly onto the bag. Crumples came up behind him as he tried to get up and pressed him back down into the pavement with his foot.

"You see, Pat," said Crumples, "you could have had it all. I offered you my support, and you threw it back in my face. I would have made you a real hero. But now I think *I'll* be the hero." He leaned down and put both hands on the box within the bag. Pat gripped it harder. Crumples withdrew one hand—then punched Pat hard in the stomach. Pat let out a low moan, and couldn't help weakening his grip on the box. Crumples put both hands back on it and ripped it out of his grasp.

"NOOOOOO!" Pat cried.

Crumples smirked down at him. *"Yes,"* he said, and turned away triumphantly with the box.

Eddie and Mo ran to Pat's aid. There were tears rolling down his cheeks.

"It's okay, Pat," said Mo, "it's okay."

"IT'S NOT OKAY!" Pat exploded. "He's taking it . . . he's taking it!"

Crumples, now standing by his car, laughed back at them. "Ah, stop your moaning! You're only a bunch of kids anyway! You should be tucked up in bed!" He set the wooden case down on the hood and gazed down at it, his eyes wide with excitement.

"The head of Oliver Plunkett," he whispered, "saved by *Belfast Telegraph* reporter!"

He gently lifted the top of the case and held his breath as he prepared to look down at the miraculously preserved head of the ancient saint.

"NNNNOOOOOOOOOOOO!"

Crumples suddenly swiped the case off the hood and it cracked down onto the tarmac. The head rolled out and away across the road. Except it wasn't the head, it wasn't the miraculously preserved head, the head of a saint, three million euros' worth of holy head: it was a football.

Eddie, Mo and Pat stared at it as it rolled away down the road's slight incline.

They had gone to all that trouble, faced so much danger—for a football.

Crumples glared back at them. "What have you done with it?" he demanded. But he could tell from their own shocked faces that they were as much in the dark as he was. He smashed his fists down on the hood of his car. "I *hate* kids!" he yelled. "You haven't heard the last of this!" Then he climbed back into his car and started the engine.

Gary suddenly appeared back at Eddie's shoulder.

"Where did you—?" Eddie began.

But Gary cut him off. "Let's move," he said urgently.

"Why, what—?"

"Move!"

They all started to run.

A moment later Crumples' car burst into flames.

Crumples tumbled out, then stood looking at it absolutely confused.

And then it exploded.

Crumples threw himself to the ground and covered his head.

Despite their terror and disappointment, Eddie, Mo, Pat and Gary burst into laughter as they ran.

"Gary—have you anything to tell us?" Eddie shouted.

"I was bored, I haven't blown up anything in ages."

"Yeah, like five minutes," shouted Mo.

As they ran off into the darkness they could still hear Crumples yelling and cursing.

The good humor did not last for very long. It was now after eleven o'clock at night and a fine rain was falling. They sheltered at a bus stop and looked miserably at each other.

"What're we supposed to do?" Pat said. "We'll never save the primate now."

Eddie sighed. "We were on the right track. He had the box. He just didn't have the head in the outbuilding."

"We can't go back," said Mo, "he'll have the security doubled, tripled. . . ."

"Why don't we just call the police?" said Gary.

"Because he's not going to keep it there now, is he?

We've just blown up his outbuilding. Correction—you've just blown up his outbuilding."

"It was a slight miscalculation," Gary said. "Besides, I got you in, didn't I? Wasn't my fault the head wasn't there."

Eddie nodded. "We all did our best. It was a brave effort." Mo and Gary nodded—but Pat didn't like where this was going.

"Is that it then?" Pat snapped. "Is that all you're going to do? Are you just going to give up?"

"What else *can* we do?" asked Mo.

"Try harder! I'm going to *Hell* over this!"

"You're not going to *Hell*," laughed Eddie, "it's only an old story, nobody believes—"

"I believe!" Pat's face was a mask of anger now. He waved a finger at Eddie. "You don't understand the power of the Church! You don't understand the power of the head! That's the problem! You never did! You were more interested in making money than saving a saint!"

"That's not fair," Eddie began. "We went out of our way to help—"

"You went out of your way and did NOTHING! Do we have the head? No we do not! Are we any closer to getting the head? I don't think so! You're all crap! You're all useless! I don't know why I bothered teaming up with you in the first place!"

With that Pat walked out into the rain.

"Pat!" Eddie shouted after him.

Mo put a hand on his arm. "I'll go after him, Eddie. Go on home, it's late, we're all tired, we'll get together tomorrow, okay?"

Eddie took a deep breath, then nodded. "Where's he going to sleep? I think the police are waiting at my house."

"Don't worry about it," said Mo. "I'll sort something out."

She squeezed his arm. "We did our best. We *are* a good team. He's just upset." She reached up then and kissed Eddie on the cheek. "See you tomorrow."

She turned and hurried out into the rain after Pat.

Eddie raised a hand to his cheek. What was she *thinking* of? In what famous gang was the leader *ever* kissed by his second-in-command?

"Are you blushing?" Gary asked, peering in at Eddie's face.

"No I'm not bloody blushing," Eddie snapped, aware that his cheeks were indeed burning. "It was the running did it, and that slap around the ear and . . . what on earth are you doing?"

Gary had turned and was running his hands over the plastic material the bus shelter was made of.

"I was just wondering how this would burn. . . ."

Eddie rolled his eyes, then walked out into the rain himself.

"See you in school," he called back.

Twenty-three

Eddie traveled to school the next morning still feeling exhausted, and rather depressed. He had been shown another glimpse of what could have been: fame and fortune—and then it had been cruelly snatched away from him. He—and his gang, of course—had done all the hard work. They'd hatched a plan, then carried it out with ruthless military efficiency, only to discover that they'd gone to all that trouble, put themselves in danger, all to steal . . . a football.

It was as if God was laughing at them.

Or if not God, then Oliver Plunkett.

Eddie sighed. What did it matter now?

Their one chance to get the head was gone.

It was time to concentrate on boring, boring, boring real life again.

Eddie wandered through the gates of Brown's Academy just as the bell rang. He spotted Ivan Cutler standing by the main doors. Boys who'd been at his party the night before, who'd eaten his food and played on his dirt bikes, filed past without speaking or looking at him.

"Ivan," said Eddie as he drew level with him, "did you all get cleared up after the party last night?"

"Huh," Ivan grunted. "They were tidying up all night. Dad was raging—fireworks landed on one of the outbuildings, blew it to bits."

"God," said Eddie. Inside he was smiling. At least they were off the hook for that.

"Dad spent hours looking through the ruins, must have been there until dawn. I mean, it was only an old outbuilding. It's not like there was anything valuable in it."

Now Eddie was confused. He had presumed that Scarface had moved the head himself, that he'd left the box in place as a way of taunting anyone who went looking for it, while hiding the head somewhere much more secure. But if he'd spent all night looking through the rubble of the outbuilding for it—it meant he really didn't have it anymore. That somebody had gotten to it before they had!

Ivan began to walk toward his first class. His father had paid for guide rails to be fitted throughout the school, so he didn't need any assistance. So Eddie turned in the opposite direction.

"Oh—Eddie. Can I borrow you for five minutes at lunchtime?"

"Borrow?"

"I just need a hand with something."

He turned away without waiting for a response. Eddie didn't like Ivan one bit, and now with the head gone he had no further reason to be friendly toward him. But he was blind, and he clearly had no other friends. What harm could it do?

Eddie managed to get through the morning without getting any further detention. He was still being watched by the teachers, but they weren't taking any direct action against him. They were probably waiting for the police report. Eddie had arrived home the night before expecting to be questioned about the fire in the school, but although they had called earlier, they hadn't waited around for him to return. Mostly because his mum spent half an hour shouting at them—*how could they even suspect her darling son of starting a fire, he was a HERO!*

But they would be back, that was for sure.

Eddie kept his head down and worked steadily through the morning. At break he made a point of eating his lunch first before searching out Ivan Cutler. He found him leaning against a wall just down from the staff common room, his schoolbag sitting lazily against his feet.

"So," Eddie said, wandering up, "what can I do for you?"

Ivan pushed himself off the wall and picked up his bag. "Can you show me which one of those is Dopey Danvers' locker?"

Eddie looked along the corridor toward the bank of lockers the teachers used for their personal possessions.

"What? Why do you—?"

"Will you just show me?"

Eddie could see through the staff room windows that it was packed. The same windows allowed the teachers to keep an eye on their lockers. Pupils were prohibited from entering the corridor during lunchtimes.

"Ivan—I really don't need another detention."

"Please. It's important. If we're caught, I can get you off. You know I can."

"But why is it imp—"

"Just do it!"

He should just tell Ivan to get lost. He should just walk away.

But he didn't. He never did.

Instead Eddie said, "All right, keep your hair on," and guided Ivan across to the lockers. Each one had a plastic name tag stuck to it, so it wasn't difficult to locate Danvers'. About half of them had small padlocks. Luckily Danvers' didn't.

"Okay," said Eddie.

"Right—now open it."

Eddie glanced behind him, saw that there was nobody watching from the staff room, then opened the door. There was a small handbag inside, and a stack of Bibles. He whispered this information to Ivan, then added: "What're you going to do, Ivan, leave her an apple?"

"No," said Ivan, reaching into his schoolbag, "I'm going to leave her a head."

Eddie staggered back as Ivan pulled the head of Oliver Plunkett from his bag. He had never actually seen the head in the flesh before—but there was absolutely no doubt what it was. It looked ancient, and scary, and, as Pat had told him, exactly like a coconut.

"You . . . you . . . you . . . you . . . ," he stammered.

Ivan merely grinned and placed the head inside the locker, on top of the pile of Bibles.

"You . . . you . . . you . . ."

Ivan shut the locker door, then lifted his bag and quickly walked away.

"What . . . what . . . what . . . ," Eddie repeated, hurrying after him, ". . . that's the head of Oliver Plunkett."

"I know what it is, you idiot," said Ivan, returning to his position against the wall.

"But . . . but . . . but . . . but . . . half the country is looking . . ."

"I know what half the country is doing. My dad stole it. And I stole it off him."

"But, but, but, but, but . . ."

"Eddie—will you settle down?"

"I . . . I . . . I . . . I'm settled," said Eddie.

"Right. Well. It's quite simple. People hate me because my dad's Scarface Cutler. When he's not slicing people up he's stealing, and when he's not stealing he's threatening people, and when he's not threatening them he's slicing them up. I *hate* my dad. And I *hate* Dopey Danvers. I'm going to scare the bloody pants off her. So I'm getting them both back, okay?"

Eddie gulped. "Okay," he said.

He stared down the hall. The head of Oliver Plunkett.

Right there in front of him. He could take it, take it right now, run, run, run, off with it. Ivan wouldn't even know the difference!

Go, Eddie, go! Open the locker! Take the head! Now or never! He started back down the corridor . . .

. . . but at that moment the bell for the end of lunch rang, the staff room door opened and the teachers began to file out. Eddie saw Miss Danvers walking with Mr. Short and Mr. Smithins at the back of the group. He quickly knelt down and pretended to tie his shoelaces. None of the teachers paid any attention to him. Danvers was just walking past—then she stopped and said, "Oh—my handbag! Just be a minute!"

Short and Smithins strolled on while Danvers hurried back to her locker. She opened the door and . . .

. . . removed her handbag. She closed the locker door and moved quickly to catch up with her fellow teachers as if nothing out of the ordinary had happened.

Eddie wondered for a moment if Danvers was as blind as Ivan. But then she stopped, and a puzzled look raced across her face.

"I . . . just . . . one . . . moment," she said haltingly. "I thought . . . I . . ."

She hurried back to her locker and opened the door.

Her mouth began to move up and down, her finger jabbed out toward the locker and she tried to speak, but words would not come.

Screams would, though.

Loud, long, horrified screams; teachers froze, pupils shuddered.

Dopey Danvers staggered back across the corridor. Then she fainted.

As she hit the ground Short and Smithins, and then most of the other teachers, rushed back to help her.

"Call a doctor!" Short shouted.

"Call an ambulance!" added Smithins.

"Miss Danvers! Miss Danvers!" yelled another.

Eddie stared at the locker. The door remained open. He could see part of the head. But nobody else was paying any attention to it. They were all so concerned for their collapsed colleague that they didn't think to check what had caused her to collapse. Even though she was surrounded by teachers, there was two or three meters of clear space between them and the locker.

Eddie, still kneeling, cautiously raised himself. He looked back at Ivan—but he had already pushed himself off the wall and was walking away, evidently satisfied with his revenge and not at all interested in the head of Oliver Plunkett.

The head of Oliver Plunkett!

All of Eddie's plans and ambitions had collapsed with his gang's failure to steal the head—but now here it was, ripe for the taking. A second chance. But he surely had only moments to exploit it.

Eddie surged forward, swinging his schoolbag off his back and opening it as he approached the locker. As he passed the group of teachers gathered around Danvers he saw that she was beginning to come round. She was muttering, "The head . . . the head . . ."

"It must be her head," said Smithins, "she must have cracked it when she fell."

"No . . . no . . . she wants the headmaster," said another teacher.

Eddie reached the locker. He hardly broke stride as he shot his hand inside it and rolled the head out, allowing it to fall into his bag before turning away, swiftly closing the flap over and buckling it shut as he moved.

Behind him Danvers got back onto her feet.

"Stay down until the doctor—" one of the teachers was saying.

"No . . . no, you don't understand . . . the head . . . the head . . ." She staggered across to the locker and pointed. "In here, it's in . . ."

And then she followed her own finger, and saw that there were only Bibles inside.

"But . . . but . . . but . . ."

She fainted again.

Meanwhile Eddie rounded the corner and let out a very quiet cheer.

Twenty-four

There weren't actually any brass bands playing on the train on the way home—but Eddie could hear them in his head. They were playing old songs like "Happy Days Are Here Again," and "Hallelujah! Hallelujah! Halle . . . lu . . . lu . . . lu . . . jah!!!!!!" He had the head of Oliver Plunkett in his schoolbag!

He deliberately chose a seat away from everyone else so that he could sneak peeks at it, and touch it, and play with its odd, coarse hair. The skin felt like old shoe leather, and sent a shiver through him, but it didn't stop him touching it again, and again—Oliver Plunkett, Oliver Plunkett, Oliver Plunkett—his name seemed to go with the rhythm of the speeding train—Oliver Plunkett, Oliver Plunkett, Oliver Plunkett.

Mo and Pat, as he had arranged, were waiting for him

outside Botanic Station. Mo was sitting on a bench, Pat was pacing back and forth. Eddie kept his face straight. He was going to enjoy this.

"Where's Gary? Did he not show up?" Mo and Pat looked at each other and shrugged. "Maybe he had to blow something up," Eddie suggested, and gave them a smile, but Mo and Pat remained dull-faced. "Well?" Eddie asked. "Did you not come up with any master plan?"

Mo glumly shook her head. She looked at Pat. "I sneaked him into my room. But he walked the floor all night trying to think of something. Luckily my dad was drunk, fast asleep downstairs, otherwise he would have brained me."

"Nothing at all?"

Pat wouldn't meet his eyes. He was miserable.

"Don't worry. Something will come up."

"Yeah, sure," said Pat.

Eddie set his schoolbag carefully down on the ground. He turned and began to examine a street map of Belfast attached to the station wall. "It's just a matter of knowing where to look. Oh," he said absentmindedly, "anyone fancy a can of Coke?"

Mo shook her head.

"Yeah, I suppose," said Pat.

"There's one in my bag."

Eddie continued to study the map. Pat stopped his pacing and bent down to the bag. He undid the straps and pulled up the flap.

There was a moment of complete shock, and then: "HOLY GOD!"

216

Eddie turned, smiling broadly. Mo, confused, got off her seat to look in the bag. Her eyes nearly bulged out of her head. *"Eddie?"*

Eddie shrugged modestly. "It's all a matter of trusting your leader," he said.

"It is . . . real . . . isn't it?" Pat asked, still stunned.

"Course it is. Smell it."

"But what . . . *how*?" Mo asked.

"Oh, I have my ways. The important thing is, we have it. Now we have to decide what to do with it."

Pat looked up, his surprise at finding the head in the bag immediately giving way to memories of the previous evening when they'd argued over its fate. "We take it to Drogheda," he said bluntly.

"Or you could give it to me."

It was quietly said, and a familiar voice. Eddie didn't even have to look up to know who it was.

A boy in a wheelchair, with twelve teen gangsters for company.

Captain Black and the Reservoir Pups.

Pat quickly closed the bag, then draped it over his shoulder. Eddie and Mo moved beside him as the Reservoir Pups formed a circle around them, allowing space only for Captain Black to maneuver his wheelchair through.

"Who are they?" Pat whispered.

"Reservoir Pups," whispered Mo.

Captain Black stopped his wheelchair before Eddie and gave him a long, hard look. If anything the gang leader appeared smaller, thinner, than Eddie remembered him, but his eyes were as cold as ice, and twice as dangerous.

"Long time no see, Eddie. How are you keeping?"

"Great," Eddie snapped back, "no thanks to you."

"Oh, Eddie, there's no need to be lippy." Captain Black pretended to look hurt. "What have I done?"

The anger boiled suddenly through Eddie. He was a hero now, he'd won back Oliver Plunkett's head—he wasn't about to take any of Captain Black's nonsense. "I'll tell you what you've done. You sent me to that school, didn't you? You think you can just manipulate people whenever you feel like it, don't you? Well, you can't. I'm not a remote-control car and I'm finished with you and your master plans."

"Is that right, Eddie?"

"Damn sure it's right! I knew you were after the head! But we got it! It's ours and we're keeping it!"

"Oh really?"

"Oh really."

"Don't you think you're a little outnumbered, Eddie?"

And of course, they were outnumbered. Heavily.

"Doesn't matter!" Eddie shouted. "We'll fight to the death. And all Mo has to do is whistle and the rest of the Andytown Albinos will be here in a minute. Then who'll be outnumbered? Eh?"

Captain Black nodded thoughtfully. "The Andytown Albinos? All the way from . . . let me see, Andytown? All the way from Andytown in one minute."

Eddie glanced nervously at Mo.

"They're only round the corner," she said quickly. "Just one whistle, that's all they need."

Captain Black shook his head; as he spoke Eddie noted that his teeth were slightly yellow. "You know, I'd love to believe you, but I really can't bring myself to. Especially as I've just discovered that there are no Andytown Albinos. They don't exist."

"Yes they do, they—"

"NO they don't." He said it with such authority that Mo fell suddenly silent. There was no point pretending. What was she going to do, whistle, and then stand there like a fool while her mythical gang failed to rescue her?

Captain Black gave a cool, thin smile. "Very well. Now, even though you are vastly outnumbered, I have no wish to cause a scene here in public. That is not the way we usually operate. Why don't you just hand the head over, and then we can all be on our way."

"No way," said Pat.

"No chance," said Mo.

"There's your answer," said Eddie.

So that was it. They were clearly going to get the beating of their lives. But they couldn't just give up the head without a fight.

"You're very brave," said Captain Black, "foolish but brave. But still, I'd prefer to settle this without having to resort to violence. What about a deal? A swap. You give me the head—I'll give you something you want."

Eddie snorted. Which wasn't pleasant, but got his point across.

"There's nothing you have," said Mo, "that we could possibly want."

"Really?" said Captain Black. He nodded behind him

and the circle of Pups split open to reveal Bacon and Bap standing about twenty meters away holding another boy between them.

Pat's mouth dropped open. "Sean?" he said. Eddie and Mo looked confused. "He's my best friend."

Sean had a black eye and the knees of his trousers were torn. He'd clearly been in a fight. "I'm sorry, Pat," Sean called, "I was only trying to help."

"Ah," said Captain Black, "friendship, it's such a wonderful thing. Found him wandering the streets, lost and hungry. He put up quite a struggle, I might add. But he's *ours*. However, he can be *yours*. In exchange for a little old head."

"You are *evil*," said Mo.

"I'm not *evil*," Captain Black laughed, "I'm a businessman, or is that the same thing? So what's it to be, Eddie? The head of Oliver Plunkett or the life of your little friend?"

Eddie wasn't ready to cave in yet. "What're you going to do, big shot," he said derisively, "*kill* him? I don't think so."

Captain Black sighed. "You're right, Eddie, we're not going to kill him. After all, we're not barbarians, are we? No, this is what we're going to do. If you don't give us the head, then we're going to hand your little friend over to Scarface Cutler. *He'll* kill him. And then he'll kill you, and you, and you. . . ." He pointed round the three of them. "This way, Eddie, your little friend gets his little friend back, you get off scot-free, and I get a nice big payoff from Scarface Cutler for returning the head. Look, everybody wins!"

220

Eddie could hardly believe it.

Once again he had managed to snatch defeat from the jaws of victory.

He was never, ever going to come out on top.

He looked back at Mo. She shrugged. He looked at Pat, still clutching the schoolbag protectively against his chest.

"It's your call, Pat. We hand the head over and get your friend, or we make a fight of it, get beaten up, lose the head and probably your friend as well."

"Put like that, I've no bloody choice, have I?" Pat rasped. He could hardly believe it either. At the very start he'd been threatened with Hell; then just a few minutes ago they'd saved the head and he'd felt like he was in Heaven. Now here was Sean. Last time they'd been together Sean had been part of a gang beating him up in the school dormitory.

But that was in the past.

Clearly their friendship was still important to Sean. He'd come all this way, to a strange city, to try to help him.

Friendship or Hell.

That was Pat's choice.

Hell or friendship.

But it was really no choice at all.

He stepped forward and thrust the bag toward Captain Black. "Take it," Pat snapped, "and I'll see you in Hell."

Twenty-five

Pat was never sure, later, what made him hesitate at the very, very, very, very, very last moment as he went to hand over the head of Oliver Plunkett to Captain Black and the Reservoir Pups.

Something in the air, a forewarning that something was about to happen, a voice in his head, saying, hold on, Pat, the show's not over yet.

But he did, he hesitated, it was only a fraction of a second; he was reaching the schoolbag out; Captain Black had opened his arms to accept it; time seemed to freeze; he could almost see the excitement emanating from the gang leader; he was feverishly aware of the despair in Sean's eyes, and the heartbreak of Eddie and Mo weighed heavy on his arms; around him pedestrians passed by unaware of the drama being played out; traffic trundled past on the road; passengers continued to stream out of Botanic Station, businessmen coming home early from work, shoppers weighed down with plastic bags, other pupils from Brown's Academy walking quickly, embarrassed by the color of their blazers but frustrated at trying to cross the road because the lollipop man was nowhere to be seen . . . No, there he was, against the wall behind Sean, enjoying a sneaky cigarette, but he was finished now, he was lifting his six-foot metal lollipop, going back to work . . . No, *whacking* one of the boys holding Sean with it . . . then *smashing* the other one.

Eddie let out a whoop as his body-washing friend and now lollipop man Barney suddenly attacked Bacon and Bap from behind. The two Pups reeled away, leaving Sean momentarily free.

Even as Captain Black's hands began to curl round the straps of the schoolbag with the head inside, Pat yanked it away.

"Into the station!" Barney yelled at Sean, who didn't need a second invitation; he charged away down the sloping walkway toward the platform.

"Give me the—!" Captain Black screamed and the circle of Pups began to close around Eddie, Mo and Pat.

But Barney wasn't finished. He plowed into the Pups, swinging his lollipop above his head like he was an ancient knight or Conan the Barbarian. The Pups who were left standing scattered away out of the reach of this bizarre man with his strange weapon.

"Go, Eddie, now!" Barney shouted.

Eddie, Mo and Pat raced into the station after Sean. As soon as they passed the entrance Barney positioned himself there to try to prevent any of the Pups from giving chase. They attacked, and they attacked again, but Barney stood firm.

Sean was waiting for them down at the platform. Pat stood beside Eddie, not sure what to say to his old friend. They only had to wait a few minutes for the next train to arrive, but it was the longest few minutes of their lives. They looked at each other, panting hard, hardly able to believe what had happened, and then back up the ramp toward the station entrance, which was out of sight. But they could hear the sounds of battle. The yells and shouts and curses. The cries of pain.

Then the train was there, easing casually to a stop, as if it was unaware of being the most important train in the history of the world. Or something like that.

They jumped on board and sat staring at the doors, willing them to close, praying for them to shut before Barney was overwhelmed, before the Reservoir Pups came streaming down the walkway.

And—just like that—they began to close.

And then they were completely closed.

Then they were moving.

And yes . . . there the Pups finally were, charging down the walkway, screaming and yelling and pointing and some of them were thumping the side of the train as it passed, but they were too late, TOO LATE!

In the train high fives were the order of the day.

Hugs and dancing and shouts and screams of excitement and relief; other passengers looked on like they were mad. And they were, mad with relief, mad with thanks for Barney, mad because they had lived through a mad adventure, they had survived!

When they had finally calmed down they decided to get off three stops along, close to the Falls Road, and therefore beyond the Reservoir Pups territory. This was an area controlled by a gang called the Real Pups— former members of the Reservoir Pups who'd either fallen out with or been thrown out of Captain Black's gang; they were a small but strong outfit who would rather die than allow any Reservoir Pups into their territory. Mo, who was familiar with this part of the city, led them out of the station and about a hundred meters along the road toward a red-bricked building attached to a small church.

"Father Patrick," she explained. "I've known him all my life. He'll know what to do."

Eddie agreed. They had the head now, but the longer they held on to it, the more danger they would be in. They had to get rid of it, get it back to where it belonged. Eddie felt exhausted, too tired to even think about demanding a reward or whether he would get to star in the movie version of their adventures, which was bound to happen. He just wanted it over with. As they drew closer to the church Eddie took off his blazer, rolled it up, then threw it into a rubbish-filled bin sitting at the side of the road.

"What're you doing?" Pat asked.

"I'm finished with that school," said Eddie. "Captain Black made me go there. It's the last time he makes me do anything."

Mo smiled supportively. "You can join me, Eddie, come to my school."

Eddie had never even thought about what school she went to. "Which one's—?"

"The school of life. Out on the streets, Eddie, doing what we do. If we can beat the Reservoir Pups we can beat anyone. We don't need school. We need to make our own rules. Do our own thing. You know, there's enough gangs out there to get together to take on the Pups, it just needs someone to bring them together. We could do that, Eddie. *You* could do that."

Eddie could hardly make a ham sandwich without slicing his finger off, but it was good to know that somebody believed in him. So he smiled and shrugged, then nodded for Mo to approach the front door of the house at the side of the church. Behind them, Sean tugged on Pat's sleeve. When Pat looked back, Sean said: "Sorry. About all that . . . stuff . . . at school."

"Sorry too," said Pat.

And that was it. Simple. They smiled at each other.

Mo rang the doorbell and stood back. After a few moments a small, elderly, rather portly priest answered it.

"Hello, how can I—"

"Hello, Father Patrick."

The priest peered a little closer, and then he smiled keenly. "Mo! How are you?" And then he quickly examined the rest of them. "And with little chums as well! Come in, come in—I've just put the kettle on."

With that the priest turned and led them through his small, neat parish house to a living room which smelled of mothballs and whiskey. Although it was a warm day a fire glowed in the hearth. There were photographs all around the walls of Father Patrick at various church functions. Mo quickly introduced Eddie, Pat and Sean, but before she could explain the reason for their visit, he disappeared into the kitchen. He shouted back, "I hope you like Jaffa cakes!"

Pat sat in an armchair and hugged the schoolbag protectively. Sean sat beside him on one of the arms. Mo and Eddie sat side by side on a small couch. Father Patrick quickly reappeared with the tea and a new box of Jaffa cakes.

"Ah, Mo," he said somewhat wistfully, "it's so good to see you. Tell me, what have you been up to—any more slates come your way?" Mo smiled sheepishly. Father Patrick read the confusion on Eddie's face and said, "A few months ago some boys from one of the local gangs stole the slates from the church roof. Mo here stole them back, didn't you?" Mo shrugged. Father Patrick passed the box of Jaffa cakes to Eddie; he took three and passed it along the line. "But tell me now, Mo," said Father Patrick, "what seems to be troubling you, you're not just here to visit an old man, I can see that by your faces."

"We brought you a present," said Mo.

Father Patrick looked surprised. "Me . . . ?" The box of Jaffa cakes had now arrived back with him; he bit into one and looked expectantly at Mo.

Mo nodded across at Pat, who, for several moments, didn't move, but instead clutched the bag a little tighter, as if he wasn't prepared to let it go.

"Pat," said Eddie, "it's time. . . ."

Pat finally nodded. He held the bag out to Eddie, who undid the straps, but left the flap closed. He placed it at Father Patrick's feet.

Father Patrick looked at it curiously. "Now I hope there's not a kitten in here, people are always bringing me kittens." He lifted the flap. "Seem to think that because I live alone I need to have a pet, but they never ask whether I'm allergic to—"

He stopped suddenly. He had a florid face, but the color drained out of it instantly. "My . . . my . . . my . . . ," he stammered. He looked up at Mo. She nodded. He hesitantly reached into the bag and allowed the tips of his fingers to touch the top of Oliver Plunkett's head—and immediately he shot back in his chair as if he'd been electrocuted.

Surprised, Eddie crushed the Jaffa cake in his hand.

"My God almighty!" exclaimed Father Patrick. "It was like touching . . . it was like touching . . . I don't know what it was like touching. It was . . . powerful."

Eddie looked from Mo to Pat and back to Father Patrick. They had all touched the head, and none of them had felt anything unusual. And something else—Eddie shivered— the room felt suddenly cooler. There was no breeze, no draft, but the fire had gone out. Perhaps it had died naturally. Perhaps it hadn't. Although Eddie knew it wasn't possible, Mo had actually gone a little whiter. It was the first time

228

either of them had considered that there might be something truly miraculous about the head.

"Mo . . . Mo . . . ," said Father Patrick, "where did . . . how did . . . ?"

"We stole it back from the people who stole it," said Mo.

Father Patrick shook his head—not Oliver Plunkett's—in disbelief. Between them they then told Father Patrick their story; he clapped his hands together and laughed and let out whoops of excitement as their tale unfolded. Gradually the room began to warm again. When they had finished they sat back and Father Patrick looked around them in wonderment. "This is incredible . . . fantastic . . . the primate, the pope. My goodness, Mo, Eddie, Pat, Sean, you'll all be made saints!"

He rose to his feet then. "And now, if you don't mind, I've got some phone calls to make!"

He left the room and clumped excitedly up the stairs, and then they heard the muffled sound of his voice as he called whoever he had to call.

The head of Oliver Plunkett remained in Eddie's schoolbag, but after seeing Father Patrick's reaction to it, none of them dared touch it again.

Half an hour passed. They demolished the Jaffa cakes. Eddie and Mo talked in hushed whispers about what reward they might possibly get and what they should say to reporters and what Eddie's mum would think and if it would mean big trouble for Mo's dad.

"Are you worried about going back to the orphanage?" Sean asked Pat.

Pat shrugged. "I don't want to ever go back."

"Maybe once this comes out, we'll be adopted."

"I don't even want to be adopted."

Sean nodded in agreement. "You've done a great thing, Pat. I'm proud of you."

"And you did an even braver thing. You came after me, to look after me, even though I did a bad thing."

"It's done now. We're friends again."

They both nodded.

Father Patrick's voice continued to sound from upstairs. They grew bored, their talking stopped. Gradually, one by one, they began to nod off to sleep.

When the doorbell rang Eddie was the first to wake up. He shook himself. He wasn't sure how long he'd been asleep, but it was already starting to get dark outside. He heard Father Patrick's rapid footsteps on the stairs. Eddie woke the others and then they waited together as the sound of muffled voices drifted in from the front door. After another few minutes the living room door swung open and Father Patrick entered, followed by a tall, imperious-looking priest.

"Children," Father Patrick said, "isn't it wonderful? Bishop Tuohey has driven all the way from Drogheda to collect the blessed head of Oliver Plunkett."

Pat felt his blood run cold.

The bishop who had cursed Pat to Hell.

Tuohey stepped into the room. He snapped his fingers. "The head, show me the head."

Eddie, who had no idea about Pat's previous encounters with the priest, but could see his young ally's unease, didn't move. But Mo, unaware of it all, reached into the bag and lifted out Oliver Plunkett's head. She carefully handed it to the bishop, whose eyes widened as he reached for the head. But as soon as he touched it, another jolt of *something* seemed to pass through his body. His face blanched, sweat cascaded down his brow. He almost dropped the head. But then whatever it was seemed to pass, and the bishop recovered most of his haughty poise.

"That was . . . this is . . . *fantastic* . . . ," he said. "Such . . . incredible . . . force . . ." He looked around the four kids. "And you got this back all by yourselves?"

Eddie nodded.

"And nobody else knows about it?"

They shook their heads.

"Well, I'm full of . . . admiration." He smiled, but it came from a face not used to smiling, and it didn't look quite right. As if he was aware of this himself, Bishop Tuohey immediately dropped the smile and turned to Father Patrick. "Father—might I talk to the children in private?"

"Yes, yes, of course, I'll just tidy up here . . . get right out of your way."

Father Patrick quickly picked up the tray of teacups and the plate which had once contained a full box of Jaffa cakes and retreated into the kitchen. He closed the door firmly and a moment later the sound of a radio playing hip-hop music drifted out.

Bishop Tuohey nodded around the four friends.

"I take my hat off to you all," he said, although he didn't have one. "I never would have thought it possible." He cleared his throat. "However, Father Patrick didn't quite get his facts right. I didn't drive up from Drogheda. I was already in Belfast. In fact I didn't drive here at all, because I have my own driver." He turned suddenly and opened the door to the hall. "Oh, driver, would you come here a moment?"

He stepped back then to allow Scarface Cutler to enter the room.

Twenty-Six

E ddie didn't know whether to laugh or cry. He felt like doing both. He'd never met Tuohey before in his life, but it didn't take a genius to work out that if a bishop hung around with someone like Scarface Cutler, then there was something not quite right about the bishop.

"What's he doing here?" Eddie demanded.

"Don't you listen?" said Tuohey. "He's my driver."

"He stole the head!"

"That's what I said. He drove down to Drogheda and stole the head for me."

Scarface Cutler strode suddenly across the room and grabbed Eddie by the front of his school shirt. He hauled him out of his chair and held him up to his face, leaving Eddie's feet dangling in the air.

"*You* stole the head from *me*," Scarface snarled.

"It was an accident," Eddie said weakly.

"You blew up my outbuilding!"

"No . . . no . . . no . . . yes . . . yes . . . yes, but I also saved your son, that's got to be worth something."

Scarface didn't even blink. "So what?" he snapped.

And there was really no answer to that. Eddie's legs flailed helplessly. Holding him now with one hand, Scarface dipped his other hand into his jacket pocket and produced a small black object. He pushed a button on it and then held the switchblade against Eddie's cheek.

"I ought to—"

"You leave him alone!" Mo shouted. She sprang up from her chair and aimed a kick at Scarface. But he merely laughed, then kicked her right back and she went tumbling away across the room. Pat and Sean, who'd been preparing to attack as well, instead went to her aid, which left Eddie still hanging in the air with the blade now beginning to bite into his cheek. He felt a trickle of something warm. It was either blood or his nose was running sideways. He suspected it was blood.

But then there was a hand on Scarface's arm. "Not now," said Tuohey. Scarface hesitated, then nodded and removed the blade from Eddie's face and lowered him to the ground. "Deal with the old guy first."

Two more of Scarface's gang appeared in the doorway behind them. "Take them to the van," Scarface snapped, "but don't harm them. That's my job."

The first hood grabbed Eddie and roughly propelled him toward the second, who began to march him outside. They did exactly the same with Mo, who was bent over almost double with pain from the kick she'd received to the stomach. Sean and Pat soon followed. Pat was the only one who put up any further resistance. As he passed Bishop Tuohey, who was holding the head up to the light and examining it with relish, he said, "Why? Why are you doing this?"

"Well," said Tuohey, "it's kind of fun, wouldn't you say?"

"How's it fun?" Pat shouted, doing his best to stand firm as one of the hoods dragged him toward the door.

"How?" said Tuohey. "Well, I get to mastermind a famous robbery, I get to embarrass a primate who has never shown any appreciation of my hard work, I get to see him lose his chance to become pope, indeed, I become the primate, and in a couple of years, I become the pope, and I think that would be rather fun, don't you? And just for extra fun, I get to dispose of dirty little orphans like you."

"You're mad!" Pat yelled.

Bishop Tuohey gave that a moment of consideration, then nodded. "It certainly helps." Then the hood kicked Pat in the shins and yanked him hard toward the door.

Bishop Tuohey turned his attention to the kitchen, where Father Patrick was still listening to the radio, blissfully unaware of the drama being played out in his living room. Scarface came up beside him.

"No witnesses," said Bishop Tuohey.

"No witnesses," agreed Scarface Cutler, raising his switchblade and moving toward the kitchen door.

"No witnesses," Pat whispered in the back of the van taking them to God knows where, "no witnesses. I heard him."

"That means—" Sean began.

"It means," Eddie cut in, "no witnesses, it means . . ." and he made a cutting action across his throat.

Mo massaged her stomach. "They can't kill us," she whispered, "we're only kids."

"Yeah, right," said Eddie.

"Shut up in the back," one of the hoods shouted.

"Shut up yourself, face-ache," Sean shouted back.

"Shhh," said Mo.

"What's the difference," asked Sean, "if they're going to kill us anyway?"

"They could kill us . . . *harder*," said Eddie, "*sorer*, more *longly* . . ." He was looking for the right word, but he wasn't quite there. He blew air out of his cheeks.

Mo was looking at him. "What are we supposed to do?" she whispered.

Eddie looked from her to Pat, and then Sean. They were all looking at him. He had proclaimed himself leader of their gang, and now it was up to him to prove it.

And he would have, except he didn't have the faintest notion. They were trapped in the back of a locked van, being taken to their doom by big guys with knives, and probably guns. The only thing Eddie could think of was getting down on his knees and begging for their lives. It wasn't very heroic, and it wasn't very likely to be successful.

Bishop Tuohey was planning on being the next pope. He would control millions—billions of people across the planet. He wasn't going to let anything stand in his way, least of all two orphans on the run, one girl who was supposed to be living in exile in Scotland because her dad was

236

just out of prison, and Eddie Malone, a tearaway suspected of burning down part of his own school.

Who was going to miss four kids like that?

His friends were still waiting for some sort of response from Eddie, but none was forthcoming. The only sound was that of the rain hammering against the roof of the van and the splash of its tires through the sodden streets of Belfast.

Eventually the van veered to the left, and Eddie just caught a glimpse of two familiar gateposts through the front window. They were pulling into the driveway leading up to Scarface Cutler's house. For a moment he was confused, because if Scarface was going to kill them, then why bring them home—but then he remembered that Cutler believed in the ethos of hide in plain sight—if you want to do something bad do it where they'll least suspect you of doing it, right in your own backyard. Just as he had brought Oliver Plunkett's head home before.

The van raced up the drive and around to the back of the house, parking alongside one of the remaining outbuildings. As they were bundled out into the now torrential rain and ripping wind, Eddie could see paper plates, the remains of burgers, crisp bags and wrapping paper being hurled about. Off to the left were remnants of the outbuilding they'd blown up the previous night. Eddie looked hopefully up toward the main house; several windows were lit, but it was difficult to make out any detail through the thick curtain of rain. They all jumped as lightning tore through the night sky.

"Get them in!" Scarface shouted.

One of his gang pushed and prodded them toward the outbuilding doors; another opened them up and switched on a light. There was a pile of disused furniture and cardboard boxes inside. As Scarface followed Bishop Tuohey inside, he closed the doors after him. Immediately the sounds of the storm were cut off, as if God himself had turned off the rain tap and stopped blowing cold air. Eddie knew now that even their screams would not be heard up at the main house.

Chairs were pulled down from amongst the pile and Eddie, Pat, Sean and Mo were forced down into them. Scarface's two comrades stood over them with guns while Scarface himself and Bishop Tuohey conferred in whispered tones in a corner. Eddie looked helplessly at Mo. He still hadn't come up with a master plan. He was willing to listen to Mo's master plan. He was willing to listen to Pat's or Sean's or even to the small dead mouse lying in the corner if it had a plan, or the moth batting frantically against the bare lightbulb. But it seemed that nobody had a plan.

The fact was, they were going to be killed.

But if they're going to kill us, why give us chairs?

Because they don't want us running around when they start shooting.

He wondered where their bodies would be buried.

He touched his foot against the cement floor. It wasn't soft, but it looked as if it had only been laid recently. *Perhaps under here. Perhaps each time Scarface kills someone, he buries the body right here, then puts on a fresh layer of cement. Perhaps . . .*

"You must be wondering," Bishop Tuohey said, coming

238

forward into the light, "how we're going to kill you. Whether we're going to shoot you, or carve you up with a knife, or smack you with a hammer until your heads are flat and your bones are crushed?"

"Or you could just keep talking," Pat said, "and bore us to death."

Pat, it seemed, was determined to go out fighting.

Bishop Tuohey's hand flashed out and struck Pat hard across the cheek; Pat shot backward, toppling out of his chair. Eddie jumped out of his, determined to at least put up a struggle before he was killed. Sean joined in, then Mo followed suit. Four of them against four grown men, two of them with guns.

Before any of them could land a blow Scarface stopped them in their tracks with a thunderous yell.

"STOP THIS!"

His blade cut through the air and stopped a millimeter from Eddie's throat.

Eddie gulped.

"NOW SIT DOWN!"

They sat.

It was the briefest rebellion in the history of brief rebellions.

"Oh, children," said Bishop Tuohey, shaking his head, "you must learn to be patient. The truth is, you see, that we have decided against the gun or the knife or the hammer. We have, instead, settled on this. . . ."

He turned then and they saw for the first time that Bishop Tuohey had brought Eddie's schoolbag with him from the priest's house. It no longer contained the head, which was now sitting on a table, almost neglected, at the back of the outbuilding. The bishop delved inside the schoolbag, and very carefully, using his bunched fists rather than his fingers to lift it, he withdrew the empty box of Jaffa cakes from Father Patrick's house.

The empty box of Jaffa cakes.

They stared at it, utterly confused.

"I don't . . . under—" Eddie began.

"It's quite simple—Eddie, isn't it?" Eddie nodded vaguely. He couldn't take his eyes off the box. "We're not complete monsters, after all. You see, shortly I will return to the scene of Father Patrick's unfortunate murder—and he is dead, believe me—where I will discover the body and alert the police. As part of their search for his murderer they will perform a postmortem on his body, they will analyze the contents of his stomach and discover that he was eating Jaffa cakes shortly before his death. Forensic examination of his living room will discover Jaffa cake crumbs on every seat. They will conclude that the priest therefore shared Jaffa cakes with four other people—his killers. But it will take several days for them to come to this conclusion. They will then race around to his house to search for the packet of Jaffa cakes in the hope that it will—and it certainly *will*—carry the fingerprints of his killers. But they won't find the packet, because I will have cleared the house of foodstuffs, fearing that they might go off. They will come to me and say, Bishop Tuohey, did you find a packet of Jaffa cakes when you were clearing the kitchen, and I will say no, I don't think so, and I will pretend to search the foodstuffs I removed. As far as the police are concerned, I won't find it—but I will have it, safely under lock and key, so that if at any time in the coming days, weeks, months or years you breathe a word about my involvement in the theft of the head of Oliver Plunkett, I will suddenly produce the box of Jaffa cakes, and you will all be sent to prison for the rest of your lives for murder."

Eddie, Mo, Sean and Pat stared at him, quite, quite stunned, while Bishop Tuohey grinned triumphantly. His plan was audacious, fiendish, simply breathtaking.

Even Scarface looked stunned. He turned to Bishop Tuohey and said: "Can't we just whack them with a hammer?"

"No," said Biship Tuohey.

"Beat them with a brick?"

"No."

But Scarface wasn't to be denied. He pulled himself up to his full height. He flashed his blade through the air again. Then he turned to Bishop Tuohey and shook his head. "Look, Bishop, the Jaffa cakes thing is clever, but it's a bit complicated. Really, believe me, you're new to this game, but I've been doing it for years. Complicated things always fall apart, it's like buying a bike with ninety-six gears, you only really need five or six. Honestly, just let me slit their throats and bury them here, it's much simpler."

Bishop Tuohey rolled his eyes. "Oh all right then. But just make it quick. I hate the sight of blood."

Scarface grinned, raised his switchblade, and moved toward Eddie.

Twenty-seven

There is a popular phrase which is widely overused, but which is quite appropriate here.

Often when you are racing to the cinema to see a movie but get caught up in traffic or there's a huge queue to get in, but you finally make it with moments to spare before the start of the movie, you say you got there in the *nick of time*.

When you've been sent to the shop but you get waylaid playing computer games in the arcade, and you're on a winning streak, but you realize that the shop is going to close in exactly three minutes and your mum will ground you for a hundred years if you don't get what she sent you for, and you have to race to get there, jumping over cars, swinging across crocodile-filled rivers, crossing roads before the green man comes up, but just make it, you get there in the *nick of time*.

That is the popular phrase, and it is quite an apt one for this scene. Because as Scarface raised his switchblade to slice at Eddie's throat, his bloodthirsty eyes wide with excitement, with Mo screaming, "Nooooooo!" in the background—the outbuilding door was suddenly flung open and they all turned to find Scarface's wife, Ivan's mum, standing there with a shotgun raised and saying: "Put down that knife!"—just in the nick of time.

Lightning jagged out behind her and rain swept through the doorway on great gusts of wind.

"Put it down, I say!"

Scarface, understandably, looked annoyed. "But, darling—"

"Drop it!"

"Darling, you've never complained before!"

"This is different! Now put it down or so help me I'll blow your head off!"

Scarface slowly lowered the knife. Then he dropped it completely. Mrs. Cutler waved the gun at his two comrades, and they too dropped their weapons.

Bishop Tuohey backed away. "What's going on? I don't understand. . . ."

"You wouldn't," said Scarface, "you're not married . . . just do what she says."

"But I'm a bishop, I don't have to—"

"Shut your cake hole, Bishop," warned Mrs. Cutler. Tuohey fell silent. Mrs. Cutler nodded at Eddie. "You, kids, open that cupboard. There are ropes, tie them up, tie them up good and proper."

Eddie's heart was thumping at a hundred miles an

hour, but he didn't need another invitation. None of them did. They happily jumped to their task. Scarface tried talking his wife out of it, but she wasn't having any of it. Eddie thanked her. Mo thanked her. Sean and Pat thanked her, but she didn't respond, just stood with a cool, determined look in her eyes and her shotgun trained variously on her husband, his helpers and the bishop.

When they had finished, and the four men were tied up, sitting on the floor, Sean stepped forward and slapped Bishop Tuohey hard across the face. Tuohey opened his mouth to yell at him—and Pat stuck the dead mouse in it.

"Chew on that," he growled.

It was cruel and horrible and disgusting, but—so what?

Eddie turned to Mrs. Cutler. "We should call the police, we have to get the head back to—"

"You'll do what I say!" Mrs. Cutler shouted. And suddenly she didn't look at all like their rescuer. Now she was waving the gun at *them*.

Eddie was staggered by this. He had thought they'd been saved in the *nick of time*, but now he could see that her eyes were every bit as wide and mad as her husband's had been when he was about to cut their throats.

Mrs. Cutler moved cautiously past them, covering them with the gun all the time, and bent awkwardly to pick up Oliver Plunkett's head. With it lodged firmly under her arm, she then forced Eddie, Pat, Sean and Mo back out into the rain—and there they found Ivan, sitting soaked in a wheelchair, minus his sunglasses for once—and very clearly asleep.

No—not asleep, nobody could sleep through such a storm. Unconscious.

"What have you done to him?" Eddie shouted against the great booming rolls of thunder and the hammering torrents of rain. "What have you done?"

But she wasn't listening. She knelt behind the wheelchair and extracted what appeared to be a length of electric wire connected to a small television aerial. She thrust it into Eddie's arms.

"Take this!" she yelled, then turned and pointed at a huge old tree beside them. "I want you to climb to the top!"

Eddie didn't mind climbing trees normally, in fact back in his old home in Groomsport he'd considered himself quite expert at it. But he didn't climb trees in thunderstorms. And he certainly didn't climb trees with TV aerials in his hand—in a lightning storm? It would be like inviting God to burn him to a crisp.

"No way!" Eddie shouted. "No way! I don't care what you're up to, but there's no way I'm—"

She raised the shotgun. It was only about six inches from his face. "Do it!"

"No."

Even in the dark he could see her finger curling around the trigger. "DO IT!"

His legs felt both weak and heavy. If he agreed he doubted he could even climb the tree. "I *can't*—" he started to say, but then Mo was beside him. "Give me it," she said, and quickly snapped the electric wire and TV aerial out of his hands.

"Mo, no! It's too dangerous!"

She moved to the base of the tree, then looked back at Mrs. Cutler. "If I do this—you'll let us go?"

"YES!"

Mo began to climb.

Pat and Sean came up behind Eddie. "Seems like an awful lot of trouble to go to, to get a better picture on your TV," said Sean.

Eddie wasn't sure if Sean was joking—but he was sure that that was the very last thing on Mrs. Cutler's mind.

Because there was something terribly familiar about this.

Something he had witnessed only the night before—upstairs in the house behind him, on the television Mrs. Cutler had been watching.

Mo suddenly let out a shout as she lost her footing on one of the lower branches. It was a big tree, and under normal circumstances it wouldn't have been particularly difficult to climb, but it was rain soaked and slippery; the wind was whipping the smaller branches back at her, and more than once bolts of lightning flashed past—each time a little closer, like celestial sharks circling for the kill. She rested for a moment, then took a deep breath and climbed on.

After several more minutes of dangerous ascent she shouted down:

"Is this high enough?"

"Higher! Higher! To the very top!"

Mo gritted her teeth, girded her loins, prayed to God, cursed, did all the things that brave people do in frightening situations, then climbed on, one inch at a time, one foothold, one jagged branch. Slowly, slowly, she reached the top of the tree and jammed the aerial in between two of the highest branches.

"Make it secure!" Mrs. Cutler yelled.

Mo pulled to make sure it was safe, then began to climb back down the tree, which in some respects was even harder—and more dangerous. First of all, she was going backward; second of all, the storm was gaining strength; third and most dangerous of all, she was still carrying the electric wire, unwinding it slowly as she descended. If the lightning went anywhere near the TV aerial she would be fried in an instant.

Down below, Eddie, Sean and Pat watched helplessly. There were things they could and should have done: Mrs. Cutler's attention was mostly on Mo in the tree, they could have run away, they could have hidden or escaped. But they stayed where they were, frozen with fear or loyal to Mo, it didn't matter. They stayed.

Mo finally reached the lower branches of the tree, then jumped the last few meters; she misjudged the slipperiness of the grass at its base and went sliding onto her ear. Eddie moved to help her—but Mrs. Cutler blocked him with her gun.

"The wire!" she shouted at Mo. "Bring the wire!"

Mo pulled herself up and trailed the wire across to Mrs. Cutler, who quickly took hold of the end of it, which was already divided into two separate strands. She then placed the head of Oliver Plunkett on her son's lap, and began to press the ends of the wires into the dead eyes of the Irish saint. She was soaked to the skin, her fingers cold and shaking, so she had some difficulty in getting the slippery wires into the skull, but finally they took hold.

"What are you doing?" Mo yelled.

"I've prayed for eight years for a miracle!" Mrs. Cutler screamed. "Now at last he has sent me this head! He has shown me how to cure my son!"

Eddie had guessed already—but now the full horror of it dawned on Mo and Sean and Pat. They looked from the head to Ivan to the tree to the aerial to the lightning slicing through the sky.

"She'll kill him!" Sean shouted.

"You'll burn him to a cinder!" yelled Pat.

"No! This is God's will!" She raised her fist and shook it at the storm above. "Strike, lightning! Strike!"

"She's bonkers!" Pat shouted. "Do something!"

"She's got a bloody gun!" Eddie yelled back.

And then it struck.

A massive bolt of lightning arced across the sky and exploded into the aerial, smashed into the tree. The upper branches immediately burst into flames, the whole tree vibrated, the ground shook under them and a million volts of electricity sped down the wire and into the head of Oliver Plunkett.

Eddie, Mo, Sean and Pat turned away, determined not to see Ivan burning, but instead of the horrified screams of Mrs. Cutler all they heard was "Yes! Yes!" so they turned back and for a moment just plain didn't understand what was going on:

The head of Oliver Plunkett bathed in a weird green light.

Sparks flying off Ivan Cutler and his wheelchair.

Ivan Cutler awake and screaming, "Muuuuummmmm!"

Trying to get out of the chair, but unable to move.

Mrs. Cutler on her knees, the gun dropped in the mud, the tree burning furiously behind her, her hands clasped in prayer: "Let my son see! I pray to you, Saint Oliver Plunkett! Give him back his sight!"

"Muuummm, pleeeease!"

The wires fell away from Oliver Plunkett's eyes.

Oliver Plunkett's eyes *opened*.

Real, live, open, eyes.

Seeing for the first time in hundreds of years.

Seeing a distraught woman on her knees in the mud, praying, praying: "Please, let him see . . . let him see!"

Seeing three boys, one girl, standing with their mouths hanging open.

Seeing a man emerge from the outbuilding, throwing off the ropes that had restrained him, yelling, "What have you done? What have you done?" and running across to save his son from the huge, burning tree now falling toward him!

Eddie's eyes were fixed on the head: it was no longer just an old coconut with straw for hair. There was flesh, and blood, and eyes that saw and felt and understood. A saint come back to life.

"Let my son see!" yelled Mrs. Cutler.

The eyes swiveled in that ancient skull and fell upon Ivan.

And then the wheelchair was struck hard from behind as Scarface charged into it a fraction before the burning tree landed.

The wheelchair rolled away through the wet grass to safety, but left Scarface sprawling on the ground. He only had a fraction of a second to look up. His eyes met those of his wife and then: *whoooooosh!*

He was consumed by the burning tree.

Mrs. Cutler screamed.

"Dad! Dad!" Ivan yelled, jumping up from the wheelchair, the head tumbling out of his lap and rolling away across the grass. "Dad!"

He raced back toward the fire—not even aware that for the first time since he was a child he could now actually see. He collapsed down in the mud beside his mother and took her in his arms. "Dad!" he shouted into the inferno.

But he knew, his mum knew, they all knew that nobody could survive a fire like that.

Scarface was dead.

Ivan and his mother cried together.

There had indeed been a miracle. A wonderful, scary, ancient, ghostly miracle, but only at a price. Ivan had regained his sight, but his father had died. He was a murderous gangster, and Ivan had often said that he hated him, but he was also his father, and every boy loves his father.

Pat was the first to move. He raced across the grass and knelt down by the head of Oliver Plunkett: it now lay damp and lifeless, as if he had never come back to life at all.

250

A coconut, that was all he was now.

And yet when Pat hesitantly lifted the head he felt a distant warmth as he touched it, a hint of what had been, but it quickly faded.

He turned with the head and crossed back to his friends. "Come on," he said, "we have to go. . . ."

Eddie looked down at Ivan and his mum, comforting each other in the glow of the burning tree, then nodded. There was nothing they could do. The four of them turned and walked away, and they were soon swallowed up by the storm.

Twenty-eight

They trudged along exhausted and soaked, sad, shocked, scared, traumatized, but also exhilarated and excited. In the distance, through the now slowly weakening rain, Eddie could see the nurses' apartment block beside the Royal Victoria Hospital. He could just pick out the seventeenth floor and the light from his apartment. There they would be safe, there they could recover, there they could explain to his mum the wild and dangerous course of recent events—from the tiny, least important things, like the loss of his school blazer and bag, to the huge, important, historic events like the rescue of the head of Oliver Plunkett. She would understand and sympathize. Or she would give them all a smack in the chops. It was difficult to be sure, but that was where they were going.

"It was a miracle, wasn't it?" Pat said as they walked.

Eddie shrugged. "It could have just been the shock of having all that electricity run through his wheelchair. Ivan said there was never anything actually wrong with his eyes—it was just the shock of seeing his dad slice someone up that made him blind. So maybe it wasn't a miracle."

"But Oliver's eyes opened," said Sean, "you did see that?"

They'd all seen it, but they weren't all ready to admit it. Mo said, "We saw something—but there was so much going on, could have been an optical illusion. All that electricity."

"It *was* a miracle," Pat said bluntly.

Eddie glanced at his watch. It was well after ten p.m., long after the last train for Drogheda had left.

"No more trusting anyone else," Pat said as they approached the nurses' quarters, "we take the head back ourselves."

Everyone agreed.

They took the lift up to the apartment. Eddie opened the front door and peered in: "Sorry I'm late, I got . . . Mum . . . you'll never believe in a million years what . . . Mum?"

But there was nobody at home. Eddie ushered his friends inside. It was Mo who found the note stuck to the fridge. It said *"Sorry, love, have to work double shift. Do your homework, don't go out, don't do anything stupid, see you in the morning, lots of love, Mum."*

"Well," said Eddie, "then I guess we'll just have to make ourselves at home."

•　●　•

They slept soundly, that night: Eddie in his bed, Pat on the floor, next to the head of Oliver Plunkett, Sean on the sofa in the living room, Mo crushed awkwardly—but she said, comfortably—into an armchair. They were tired beyond dreaming.

Eddie set the alarm for six so that they'd be up and away before his mum arrived home from work. But he slept through it and it was only when Mo shook him that he finally came awake. When he stumbled into the lounge he found Sean eating Frosties, and Pat on the phone. Pat looked embarrassed for a moment, then said, "Just checking the train timetable."

When they were ready to leave, Eddie stuck his own note to the fridge. *"Had to leave early—watch the news!"*

He might not have dreamed while he was sleeping, but now that he was awake he was daydreaming: about the newspapers and the books and the movies and how he was going to be hailed as a hero all over the country, all over the world. He had fantasized about world domination, but now it didn't seem necessary. His gang was small, but perfect.

When they were all ready, they walked through the early morning mist toward Botanic Station. The Reservoir Pups were a twenty-four-hour operation, so they had to proceed with caution. When they got close to the station Eddie spotted Barney already on duty outside and shouted across to see if the coast was clear; he waved them on.

They thanked him for saving them the previous day. Barney shrugged, embarrassed, and said it was no trouble.

"We got the head back," said Eddie, and pointed at the plastic bag Pat was carrying it in.

"That's nice," said Barney, but he really had no idea what Eddie was talking about.

It didn't matter. He hadn't helped them because of the head, he had helped them because he was Eddie's friend, and a good guy.

Pat bought four first-class tickets with what was left of Crumples' money and led them down the platform to wait for the train. They were going to travel in style. Sean and Pat were back to being the best of friends, playfully punching each other and making jokes. But Mo was looking quite glum.

"Are you okay?" Eddie asked.

She nodded.

"Everything's worked out great, hasn't it?"

She nodded.

"So what's wrong?"

She shrugged. "I feel sorry for Ivan. Losing his dad. My dad's a miserable old drunk most of the time, but I'd hate to lose him."

Eddie smiled sympathetically. As far as he knew *his* dad was still alive, but he hadn't seen him in so long, it sometimes felt like he was dead. He missed him.

Up ahead the train appeared. Businessmen going to Dundalk or Drogheda or Dublin for morning meetings began to crowd forward. Pat waited for the door to the first carriage to slide open, then stepped on board, followed by

Sean. Eddie was just about to join them when Mo suddenly tugged at his sleeve.

"Eddie," she said, "I don't think we should go."

"What?"

"I don't think we should go."

"*What?* Mo, this is our moment, our moment of triumph."

"No—Eddie—it's theirs." She nodded in at Pat and Sean, already seated and talking excitedly to each other. "It's their adventure, Eddie, they set out on it, they came to a strange country, they risked their lives. We just helped. They're orphans, they have nothing, this should be their time."

"Are you bloody mental or something?"

"No, Eddie. It's how it should be."

Eddie blew air out of his cheeks. "But . . ." He looked again at Pat and Sean, and down at the bag containing Oliver Plunkett's head, and sighed. He had such dreams and ambitions, but also he knew that in a strange way Mo was right. It wasn't about him and Mo and what the head could do for them. It wasn't about money and fame. It was about right and wrong, about saving an old man from embarrassment, about returning an ancient head.

"Either get on or get off," a conductor snapped, "we're trying to close the doors."

Eddie looked across at Sean and Pat, but they weren't even looking at him; then he looked back at Mo. She smiled hopefully.

Eddie sighed again and stepped back off the train. The doors closed immediately.

Mo came up and gave him a hug.

It felt quite nice, so he hugged her back.

As the train began to move Pat finally realized that Eddie and Mo weren't on board. He leapt up to a window and pulled it across.

"Eddie! Mo! What are you doing?"

"We're not coming!" Mo shouted. "Drogheda is your territory—this is our gang's! So don't come back without permission!"

Pat smiled back at her and nodded. He looked at Eddie. "Thanks for everything, Eddie." Eddie shrugged.

The train was now picking up speed. Eddie and Mo ran alongside as far as they could.

And then they were gone, disappearing into the distance.

Twenty-nine

All over Ireland, work, schools, shops, everything came to a standstill to watch the arrival of the pope. He came by helicopter, landing at Phoenix Park in Dublin and there boarding a special bus which took him along the motorway to Drogheda. The streets of the town were thronged with tens of thousands of people, and the church itself—well, you couldn't get in there for love or money. The service was being broadcast live on television all over the island, and to many other countries as well.

The primate welcomed the pope, and then took his seat for the beginning of the service. He felt old and tired and betrayed. He glanced down at the empty space where the head of Oliver Plunkett had once sat, and then at the chair where Bishop Tuohey was supposed to be sitting. But there was no sign of him either.

They're starting to desert me, he thought, *and Tuohey is the first to go. He doesn't want to be seen with me. I am an old, beaten man.* He looked up next at the pope himself, much older than the primate was, ill of body and increasingly slow of mind. Soon he would be gone. The Church needed a good, strong, leader.

Not me, thought the primate.

He listened listlessly as prayer followed hymn, hymn followed prayer. Then the pope moved forward to a small lectern to give his address. But before he could say anything he was distracted by a commotion at the top of the church. The primate looked up and was astonished to see the young orphan who'd gone missing, Pat, and his friend Sean, racing up the aisle of the church, pursued by two police officers.

"Primate! Primate!" Pat was shouting.

A hundred miles away, sitting in Eddie's apartment, Eddie and Mo were as stunned as the TV commentators as Pat and Sean were finally stopped in their tracks by the police.

"I . . . really . . . don't know what this is all about . . . ," said the commentator, "two kids have just . . ."

As the cops tried to drag Sean and Pat back, the primate jumped up from his seat.

"No! Leave them!"

The pope was looking quite incredulous.

The primate stepped down toward Sean and Pat. "Let

them go . . . let them go . . . ," he ordered, and the police reluctantly released them. The primate looked sternly down at them.

"What is it, boys?" he said. "Why do you interrupt His Holiness when he's—"

"We brought you a present," Pat said quickly, and held up his plastic bag.

The primate's brow furrowed for a moment. Hesitantly he reached for the bag. He looked back to the pope for approval—and in response received the slightest nod. The primate cautiously opened the bag and peered inside. For several moments he didn't react at all; then he said simply, "Thank you."

He patted their shoulders softly. Then he removed the head of Oliver Plunkett from the bag and held it aloft.

"It is returned!"

All around people began to stand and cheer. The pope stepped down from the lectern, and came down to examine the head. Then he blessed it. The cheering grew louder and louder.

In Belfast, Eddie tried to stop a tear from rolling down his cheek. He didn't dare glance at Mo. She was crying away, but there was no way that he was going to let himself down like that.

He was a hero, they were all heroes, and it didn't matter that he wasn't the one being carried shoulder high through the streets the way Sean and Pat would be. The fact was that he had won, he had beaten the bad guys—

for the second time—and he still had Mo for a friend. It was a dark, dangerous city, and always would be, but for a while, at least until lunchtime, it felt like a much brighter place.

COLIN BATEMAN is the author of thirteen acclaimed novels for adults—some of them, obviously, more acclaimed than others—published in the United Kingdom. *Bring Me the Head of Oliver Plunkett* is the companion to *Running with the Reservoir Pups.*

Colin Bateman lives in Ireland with his family.